W9-BXE-180

We Two Alone

STORIES

Jack Wang

HarperVia

An Imprint of HarperCollins*Publishers*

Extracts from *On the Nature of the Universe* by Lucretius, translated by Sir Ronald Melville. Copyright © 1997 by Sir Ronald Melville. Reproduced with permission of Oxford Publishing Ltd through PLSClear.

Extract from "Lines on a Young Lady's Photograph Album" by Philip Larkin, in *The Less Deceived*. Copyright © 1955 by Philip Larkin. Reproduced with permission of Faber & Faber Ltd.

Originally published as *We Two Alone* in Canada in 2020 by House of Anansi Press.

Some of the stories in this collection have appeared elsewhere, in slightly different form: "The Valkyries" in *The Humber Literary Review*, "The Nature of Things" in *The Malahat Review* and *The Journey Prize Stories 29*, "The Night of Broken Glass" in *The New Quarterly* and *Let's Tell This Story Properly: An Anthology of the Commonwealth Short Story Prize*, "Everything In Between" in *Brick*, "Belsize Park" in *PRISM International*, and "Allhallows" in *Joyland*.

FIRST HARPERVIA EDITION PUBLISHED IN 2021

Design by Elina Cohen
Illustrations by Andrea Wan

Library of Congress Cataloging-in-Publication Data

Names: Wang, Jack, 1972–author.
Title: We two alone : stories / Jack Wang.
Description: First edition. | New York : HarperVia, 2021.
Identifiers: LCCN 2020048904 | ISBN 9780063081789 (hardcover) | ISBN 9780063081796 (trade paperback) | ISBN 9780063081802 (ebook)
Subjects: LCGFT: Short stories.
Classification: LCC PR9199.4.W348 W4 2021 | DDC 813/.6—dc23
LC record available at https://lccn.loc.gov/2020048904

21 22 23 24 25   LSC   10 9 8 7 6 5 4 3 2 1

For Angelina and the Zeds

Contents

The Valkyries *1*

The Nature of Things *45*

The Night of Broken Glass *71*

Everything In Between *93*

Belsize Park *115*

Allhallows *137*

We Two Alone *155*

Acknowledgments *247*

The Valkyries

NELSON SPENT HIS DAY AS ALWAYS, IN THE BELLY OF THE laundry. Once again, Fong Man, the owner, was nowhere to be found, and Nelson had to do everything himself: churn the washer, crank the mangle, hang wet clothes by the potbelly stove on wires that ran the length of the room, and hand-press cuffs and collars, the iron heated on the same rusty stove. A lot for one boy, even if the operation was small, all the equipment old and mismatched, the dregs of other laundries that had switched to centrifugal wringers and starching machines.

At the end of the day, instead of retiring to the back room he shared with Fong Man, he set off on Pender Street. When he reached the green dome of the World Building—once the tallest building in the British Empire—he quickened his pace, eyes darting. Whenever headlights swept across him, he flinched. These days it was risky, leaving Chinatown at night. Just last month a man out on his own had been kicked and beaten. Now that the Great War was over, jobs were scarce, and angry young men were once again roving the streets, seeking rough justice.

In the West End, he scurried past row upon row of pretty little houses with wide porches until he reached Denman Arena, incandescent against the dark expanse of Stanley Park. Nelson had been here before, but tonight, for the first time, he was going to *play*. A new junior team was holding tryouts. CHALLENGE FOR THE ABBOTT CUP! the sign had read. Now that he was sixteen, he could. So he'd pulled out his old moth-eaten gear and tossed it into a laundry bag, still smelling of soda and lime, and slung the bag over his shoulder, his tube skates tied by the laces and draped around his neck. Propped on his other shoulder was the 35-cent hockey stick he had begged his mother for before she died.

Without the usual game-day throng, the arena looked desolate. Feeling like an intruder, he slipped in through the players' entrance and found his way to the dressing room. The moment he entered, eyes slid and silence fell over the room. When he took a seat along the wall, the boys nearest scooted away. He dressed quickly, eyes to himself, then hurried onto the ice, hoping to vanish into a sea of bodies. No such luck. As he circled the rink, other boys trailed at a distance like a pack of dogs in pursuit.

A man in a wool suit and a felt hat came down to ice

level, clipboard in hand. He sized up the scene, then blasted his whistle. Nelson started. The game was up.

"Give me four lines!" the man barked.

Relief put spring into Nelson's step. He flew through the skating drills, faster it seemed than anyone else. But when the man threw out a bag of pucks, Nelson faltered. One thing to shoot a tin can or a block of wood, another to corral a solid disk of vulcanized rubber. The first pass that came his way skittered under his stick; the first shot he took flipped lazily through the air. By the time the scrimmage began he was eager to make amends, but no one would pass to him. He kept finding open ice but the puck never came. So he did the only thing he could: fetched the puck himself. Once he had it, he dashed up the ice, through wide-eyed players on both sides. At the blue line he cut wide on the point and carved himself a path to the net. He saw the goalie's fearful look—the ignominy of letting him score!—and room on the far side. He leaned in and fired so hard that blood surged into his hands.

The net rippled.

Before he could even raise his arms, a cross-check sent him into the boards. After slamming his shoulder, he landed on his back, saw lights, stars. Then everything was eclipsed by a snarling, pimple-faced behemoth. None of this was surprising; it was simply life for a boy like Nelson. And because of his mother, his young, proud, beautiful mother, snatched at fifteen from the Pearl River Delta and carried an ocean away to serve the lonely men of Chinatown, one of whom had gotten her with child, Nelson had even been ill-used by his own. He always turned the other cheek, but today—

He pulled himself up. "Whaddya do that for?"

Suddenly the boy was upon him, and all the other boys too, their foul mitts in his face. Then someone grabbed him by the scruff of his sweater. Next thing he knew, he was sitting in an office across from the man in the felt hat.

The man examined his clipboard. "Did you put down your name?"

Nelson shook his head.

The man pushed his hat back, past his widow's peak, then leaned forward, hands clasped. "Look, son, you seem like a nice kid and a decent player besides. I don't have a problem with anyone who can skate fast and shoot straight. But some of those boys"—he jerked his thumb—"have got a problem, and if they've got a problem then I've got a problem. 'Cause I aim to win, and you can't win with trouble in the locker room. See what I'm saying?"

When Nelson said nothing, the man leaned back, drummed his fingers. Then he reached into his coat, pulled out a slip of paper, and pushed it across the desk. "Here's a ticket to a Millionaires game. Why don't you take it?"

Nelson stared, searching for a crack in the man's resolve. Seeing none, he snatched the ticket and left.

———

Two nights later he was back at the rink, gazing down at the massive slab of marble that was the ice. At the age of nine, on an evening when his mother had asked him to make himself scarce, he and Sammy Kong had snuck in the gate and scrabbled up to the very last row and looked out for the very first time onto that big barn of a building, all wood and naked joists. Back then, Nelson knew as much about hockey as most people in Vancouver did, which is to say very little. He was struck by the sounds: the rasp of skates, the clap of sticks, the booming report of a hard shot into the boards. He was also struck by the speed, the way the players' hair seemed to blow in the wind. But nothing compared to Fred "Cyclone" Taylor, the best player in the world, throwing the first heavy hit, which shook the whole building and brought the crowd to its feet, thunderously. Nelson had been hooked ever since.

Unlike that first time, there were now two blue lines painted across the ice, and goalies were allowed to fall to their knees, and he was close to the action—closer than he'd ever been. But the evening would stay in his mind for other reasons. During the first intermission, a man with a megaphone shuffled onto the ice and said, "Here for your entertainment, a daring bunch of hockeyists, the Vancouver Amazons!" When seven players took to the ice in wool caps and culottes, a wave of laughter swept through the crowd. Nelson sat up, unsure of what he was seeing. Was this a novelty act? As the Amazons scrimmaged—skillfully, he thought—the crowd hooted and hollered, even booed. "Go home!" a man shouted.

"This ain't no game for ladies!" Nelson felt a little riled himself. Why could *they* play when he couldn't?

To his surprise, the Amazons came out again during the second intermission and skated about doggedly as more laughter and derision rained down upon them. At one point a man wearing skates and a long blond wig jumped onto the ice, much to the crowd's delight. He stole the puck and played keep-away, and no matter how many players descended upon him, he managed to elude them, sometimes slipping the puck through an unsuspecting player's legs, as if the Amazons had become stooges in a vaudeville act. Nelson's blood rose again, only this time at the man in the wig and all the ugly faces in the crowd, the bare-toothed boys and the rough-necked men.

After the game, as he left the arena, his thoughts still jumbled by the things he had seen, he chanced upon a mimeographed sign:

CALLING ALL LADY PUCK CHASERS!
WOMEN'S HOCKEY TEAM FORMING!
TRYOUTS THIS THURSDAY AT 7:00 PM
TIME TO GIVE THE AMAZONS SOME COMPETITION!

That's when a strange, unexpected idea entered his mind.

———

Nelson slipped back to Chinatown. At that hour, storefronts were dark but tenements and alleyways teemed with life—the clacking of mahjong, the jangle and crash of Cantonese opera. Near Shanghai Alley he caught a waft of something sickly and wondered if Fong Man was home or out again in search of oblivion.

He found the back room empty. Relieved, he lay down on one of two straw mattresses shoved into a corner at right angles. In the other corner stood a metal sink, home to a few chipped bowls. To keep out the light, they had covered the windows with butcher paper. The only nod to ornamentation was a peeling wallpaper border near the ceiling—some long-ago attempt at fashion. The room had once belonged to Fong Man alone, but when he could no longer do the work himself, he had taken Nelson on.

Nelson tried to sleep, but lurid phantasmagoria kept stalking his dreams: men in wigs, women in uniforms. In the middle of the night, he turned on the one dangling bulb in the room and studied himself in Fong Man's cracked shaving mirror. Like his mother, Nelson had small, mobile features and a spare, sinewy frame. He usually wore his hair swept back; swept forward, it wasn't much shorter than the way some girls wore their hair these days, fabulously shorn. And unlike Fong Man, whiskery as a goat, Nelson had no need for a razor. What he was thinking of doing was crazy, but he wanted to play.

By morning he had sobered up, and his fantasies of the night before seemed just that, fantasies. But all day long, as he tossed batches of laundry into the wooden barrel of the washer and hauled them dripping into the double rollers of the mangle, he kept seeing that sign and yearning for something other than drudgery. When the day's work was done, he searched the back room and found Fong Man's pipe, which looked like a bamboo flute with a small doorknob attached. Nelson scraped soot from the pipe with wire and boiled a potato on the potbelly stove, then rolled the mixture into pills and went out to Shanghai Alley to peddle them. The pipe was what drained the little money they made, so it only seemed right that it give a little back. In the past, whenever news of his scheme reached Fong Man, Nelson would get a beating, but Fong Man was now too old and too far gone for Nelson to worry much any longer.

With cash in hand, he walked a few blocks west on Hastings Street to Woodward's Department Store, a four-story brick building plastered with advertising: CARPETS! OIL SKINS! FURNITURE! HARDWARE! GROCERIES! His only previous visit had been the year his mother had taken him at Christmastime, the storefront windows glittering with lights. She had walked him through every floor, delighting in his look of astonishment and shielding him from those of others. No avoiding those looks tonight, though, especially when he ventured into the ladies' section.

"How can I help you?" a shop girl asked coolly.

"I'd like to buy a wool cap and culottes," he replied, "for my mother."

The shop girl narrowed her eyes and led him across the floor. It pained him that he was obliged to buy the least expensive things he was shown, but it meant enough left over for lipstick and rouge.

The back room was still empty when Nelson returned. Under the meager light of the dangling bulb, he put on the cap and pulled out a few licks of hair. Then he painted his lips the way he remembered his mother doing, with a pucker and a roll. When he looked in the mirror, a version of his mother looked back.

———

A few nights later he set off again for Denman Arena. As soon as he was beyond the prying eyes of Chinatown, he ducked into an alley and changed in the dark, painting his face with a blind, unsteady hand. Then he scuttled past those pretty little houses in the West End, their bay windows burnished with life.

Last week, watching the Amazons, Nelson had sympathized with their desire to play and thought that girls would sympathize with him, but as soon as he hit the ice, players began to clear off, warier than even the boys—for the same reason, or so he hoped. No one could possibly think he was a boy. There were five other players, some of whom wore boys' shorts. Next to them, he looked positively girlish. At least that's what he told himself to keep from shaking.

As he skated in lonely circles, a new girl—tall, slender, darkly bobbed—stepped through the gate and onto the ice. After a few silky strides, she was waved to the bench, where she stopped adroitly on the outside edge of one skate. As she leaned over the boards, another girl cupped a hand to her ear, and the new girl turned, compelled to look. She skated over to Nelson.

"What's your name?"

"My name?"

She laughed brightly. "You've got one, don't you?"

"Um—Nellie."

She looked at him askance. "Are you wearing . . . makeup?"

His throat seized. "Maybe."

She frowned. "We want to be taken seriously, don't we?"

He nodded.

"I'm Tessa," she said, smiling. "Everyone," she said, pointing her stick as she skated away, "this is Nellie!" Slowly the others trickled back onto the ice.

A jowly, mustached man in a greatcoat and bowler appeared on the bench and pecked a finger in the air, mouthing numbers. Seven players, just enough to field a team. He gave Nelson a long, curious look but said nothing.

With only seven, that night's session was less tryout than practice, but Nelson was still a bundle of nerves. At any moment, his cap might fly off or his culottes puddle around his ankles, and the thought made him bobble more than one puck. But at fleeting moments, caught up in the joy of it all, he felt neither boy nor girl but simply a child again, playing shinny with Sammy in Stanley Park whenever Lost Lagoon froze over.

At the end of the night, the man in the bowler, Mr. George Lichtenhein—the name sounded familiar but Nelson couldn't place it—called them to the bench. "That was . . . interesting. Let's try this again next week, shall we?"

As Nelson hurried off the ice, a voice called after him: "See you next week?"

He turned. Tessa stood by the gate, a few strands of damp hair clinging to her forehead.

"Yes," he replied.

———

They were all respectable girls. That's what Nelson gathered during practice. Lucy and Abigail Smith were sisters, homely girls with long chins who skated beautiful figures in warm-up. Libby Rogers was twenty-one and married and had tended goal for a team in Fernie. The others—Thelma Woodson, Edna Lawrence, and Tessa McNally—were all in their final year at King George High School, and Nelson could picture them striding through the halls, three abreast, the seas parting for the queen and her entourage.

At the end of their second practice, Mr. Lichtenhein gathered the team around the bench and announced a game with the Amazons. A cheer went up. Loath as the Amazons might have been to take on such upstarts, they had no choice; without a league, they were simply starved for competition.

Talk turned quickly to uniforms. Whether to wear lark caps or toques and whether or not to have tassels.

"Who cares what we wear?" Tessa said. "What we need is a name."

"What about the Georgias?" someone asked. "You know, in honor of the king."

"Or the Monarchs."

"No, the Kewpies!"

Tessa grimaced. "We need something more like 'Amazons.' Something to do with strong women."

After his mother had died, blind and crazy by the end, Nelson had found himself on the street at twelve. His mother's black valise had held all his worldly possessions, including his mother's winter coat, which kept him alive on bitter nights until he was saved by the Methodist Church and sent to live for a few glorious months with one Mrs. Wilhelmina Ostermann, a squat, bosomy, pearl-haired woman whose son had been hauled off at the start of the war for *acting in a very suspicious manner.* Yet every night in her turreted Queen Anne house in the West End, she would play Wagner defiantly on her blooming Victrola. His favorite was the urgent score that went *da da-da DAA da, da da-da DAA da . . .*

"What about the Valkyries?" he said.

Seven heads swiveled. Thelma scrunched her nose. "What are Valkyries?"

Nelson swallowed. "They're women from Norse mythology. They chose who died in battle and carried them to"—he searched his memory—"Valhalla." Mrs. Ostermann had always explained the music. She had even shown him a reproduction of a painting of caped women with winged helmets, flying on horses through storm clouds and lightning.

"Women who choose their victims," Tessa said. "I like it."

Slowly the others nodded, smiled, tapped their sticks.

"What do you think, Mr. Lichtenhein?"

His mustache twitched. "The Vancouver Valkyries. It's got a ring to it."

Tessa beamed. "Then Valkyries it is."

At the end of the meeting, the coach turned to Nelson. "So, you know Norse mythology." The man raised a brow. Then he turned and left.

At the next practice, Mr. Lichtenhein assigned the girls to positions: Lucy and Abby to point and cover point, Tessa to center, flanked by Thelma and Edna on the wings, and Libby to the role that she alone was equipped to play: goalkeeper. "And Nellie," he said with a long, significant look, "will play rover."

That night, Mr. Lichtenhein ended practice by opening a large cardboard box and pulling out socks, culottes, toques (without tassels), and seven black sweaters, each one emblazoned with two yellow Vs, one on top of the other, like chevrons. "Come on, Nellie!" Tessa hollered as she and the others hurried off the ice. Nelson thanked his coach but said he had to go, avoiding once again the perils of the dressing room. At home, he threw off his old sweater and pulled on the new one and posed before the mirror. These weren't the colors he might have wished for, certainly not the maroon and single white V of the Millionaires, but a uniform was a uniform, and this one fit surprisingly well, as if it were meant for him.

———

On game day, the Valkyries took to the ice in their new bee-striped socks while the Amazons wore their now familiar beige sweaters, "VA" stitched across their chests in red. A flyer had been made, which explained the semblance of a crowd. Though few, spectators made the occasion real. Nelson lined up behind Tessa, mouth dry, his whole body thrumming. When he looked across the way, who should he see in the stands but Frank Patrick, his dark hair perfectly coifed. Frank Patrick was not just the coach of the Millionaires' one and only Stanley Cup team in 1915 but one of two brothers who had brought Denman Arena and professional hockey to Vancouver in the first place. Nelson stood there aghast. That's when the puck dropped and the Amazons blew past.

Game on, Nellie.

A few weeks ago, from high in the stands, the Amazons had looked slow, at least compared to the Millionaires, but down on the ice they were anything but. Nelson found himself chasing the puck, more than a little overwhelmed. If not for Libby's coolheaded netminding, the Amazons might have scored early and often.

Eventually, the Amazons managed to slip one past, right through Libby's pads as she dropped to her knees. That's when Nelson finally snapped to. Until that moment he had moved in a fog, dazzled by the lights, the smattering of fans, but suddenly his head cleared. As his play picked up, so did Tessa's. Now that the game was on the line they sought each other out. As time wound down on the giant electric scoreboard, she found him streaking down the left side. Recalling his first tryout, he cut wide on the point and curled toward the net and whipped the puck far side.

Ping!

Iron and out.

After the game, as the teams shook hands, Tessa said, "Rematch. Next weekend."

The Amazons looked at one another coyly. Finally, someone said, "We won't be here. We'll be in Banff."

"Playing in a tournament," added a lanky, curly-haired girl—the day's lone goal scorer. "The Western Canada *Championship.*"

"There's a Winter Carnival in Banff," Mr. Lichtenhein explained in the dressing room afterward. "They've had a tournament for a few years now. To go with the bonspiel."

"*We* should go," Tessa said.

"Do you think you're ready?" Mr. Lichtenhein asked.

"We almost beat them!" she replied. Suddenly everyone clamored.

The coach looked around, gauging the mood. Then he smiled like the cat that got the cream. "We *are* going. I've made arrangements."

The room erupted.

"Signed us up as soon as I knew we could field a team. But I wasn't going all that way to get embarrassed. Needed some proof you girls could play."

"But . . . a *championship?*" Lucy asked.

"That's just a fancy way of saying there are no other tournaments around. And a way to sell tickets. Besides, we can compete. If the Amazons are going, so should we."

"You'll do anything to beat the Patricks, won't you?" Tessa said.

That's when Nelson remembered where he had heard his coach's name before. Frank Patrick and his brother Lester were the ones who had lured Cyclone Taylor away from the Montreal Wanderers of the rival National Hockey Association, and the team's owner was none other than *Sam* Lichtenhein. The Amazons must have been the Patricks' team, and Mr. Lichtenhein—son, nephew, cousin?—must have still been feuding.

After detailing the trip, Mr. Lichtenhein said, "I'll see you all at the train station bright and early Wednesday. And let today be a lesson to you. If you want to win, you have to play the whole game"—he glanced at Nelson—"not just one period."

As soon as the coach left and the others started to change, Nelson threw on his boots and hurried out of the room. He was already a block down Georgia Street when someone called out after him through a faint swirl of snow.

Tessa came to a breathless stop. "Don't listen to him. You played great."

"No, it's not that. I have to get home."

She raised her brows. "Are those men's boots?"

He looked down sheepishly.

"You're an odd bird, aren't you?"

When he made no reply, she said, "I can't believe we're going. Your parents will let you, won't they?"

He nodded vaguely.

"Good," she said. "We can't win without you."

———

After changing in an alley, Nelson rushed home. In the back room, he reached under his palliasse and pulled out his mother's valise, dusty and wrinkled as elephant hide. Folded inside was her brown herringbone coat, and through the scent of wool and must he caught a fading note of lavender. Before she finally died, his mother had gone raving mad. Had said some dark things, confusing him for the men who had used her. In her final months, she'd been bedridden, but their "landlord," who over the years had given her many a black eye, had let them stay in their fetid little room so long as he still found ways to extract payment. When his mother was well and truly gone, Nelson asked if he could stay, but the landlord raised his fist, enraged. Nelson managed to grab only the coat and valise before bolting.

Back then, her coat had been too big; now it was short at the wrists and tight across the back, but it fit, just.

Encouraged, he dug through bins of unwashed laundry and picked out more things. Every sweater and blouse fell flat across his chest, but he saw this as a boon: the boyish figure was in, which meant he stood to be the most girlish of all.

He was standing before the mirror in a long-sleeved cotton nightgown when the bell at the front of the laundry jingled. He tore off the nightgown and shoved it into his mother's bag and kicked the bag under his palliasse, a moment before the door to the back room opened and Fong Man appeared in a Chinese robe and Western fedora, hand trembling atop his gnarled rosewood cane.

"What are you doing?" he asked.

"Nothing."

"That's what I thought. Get back to work."

"Actually, I need some time off."

The old man scoffed. "You don't work enough as it is."

Fong Man was the one who had led the war against eighteen-hour workdays, back when he was slaving away for the old Chinese kingpins. "I thought you wanted us to work *less*."

The old man grunted, then curled up on his own palliasse. "Get back to work."

The answer made Nelson burn. Who was Fong Man to say no? If anyone was now the boss, *he* was.

But again his confidence faltered. He kept imagining all the ways he might be discovered and what might happen to him if he were. It used to be Sammy's job to row out into the harbor and scoop up sacks of opium that had floated to the surface, this after they had been dumped from ships under the cover of darkness and after the rock salt to which they had been tied had dissolved. Sammy wound up floating in the harbor himself, no doubt at the hands of a rival gang. Nelson didn't want to end up like that. But each time he thought of backing out, he heard Tessa say, *We can't win without you.*

———

First thing Wednesday morning, instead of lighting a fire in the potbelly stove and setting water to boil, Nelson stole through the streets of Chinatown, stick in one hand, valise in the other. There were no cries in the market, no Freemasons outside the Chop Suey House, just motes of snow drifting through the aureoles of streetlamps. He had left a note on the front door of the laundry: CLOSED COME BACK NEXT WEEK. It would take a while for anyone to notice, and by then he'd be long gone.

Terminal Station was a wide red-brick building with white columns on nearby Cordova Street. Nelson was first to arrive. He took a seat in the marble booking hall, drawing looks, feeling exposed. But once the others appeared—first Libby, laden with gear; then the sisters, complaining of work ("I can't tell you what it took to get the time off!"); then Thelma and Edna and finally Tessa, wearing boots that made her look even taller—he felt absorbed into their ranks. His outfit looked of a piece with their cloche hats and wraparound coats, but the sight of their sticks and pads was curious enough for someone happening past from *The Daily World* to ask for a photograph. As the team lined up, Tessa clasped Nelson around the waist, an instant before the flashbulb popped.

"And who are you ladies?" the man asked, pencil poised above a notepad.

"We're the Vancouver Valkyries," Tessa said, giving Nelson a squeeze. "Mr. George Lichtenhein's amazing band of lady puck chasers!"

When the general himself arrived in his greatcoat and bowler, he marshaled his troops and marched them onto the train. As soon as the train pulled out, Nelson and all the girls except Libby, their nominal chaperone, scampered from car to car, euphoric. He remained in a state of elation through lunch, served on trembling china in a white linen dining car, but afterward his eyes grew heavy. For the past few days he had worked around the clock, soaking and scrubbing and pressing and folding until the shelves were chock-full of brown paper parcels. He had even made the midweek deliveries, early. Now all that work was catching up with him.

He drifted off in the passenger car. By the time he awoke the world was dark and the others gone; only Tessa remained on the seat across from him.

"Where did everyone go?"

She raised a finger to her lips, then pointed up. All the bunks had been lowered.

"What time is it?"

"Late. You must have been exhausted. I couldn't sleep last night, either. And I'm *still* live as a wire."

When snoring rippled the air, Tessa said, "Let's sit in the lounge car."

The invitation pleased him, and together they skulked through slumbering cars until they came to one with large windows, beyond which shone a milky spray of stars. They settled into swiveling leather armchairs.

"So, Nellie. How did you get to be such a good player?"

Nelson recalled his days of playing shinny with Sammy on Lost Lagoon. "For a while we didn't even have skates. Just slid around in our shoes. Didn't have sticks, either. Just used some hooked branches." For a few years he had used a pair of rusty clamp-on blades he had found by the lagoon. He didn't own real skates until Mrs. Ostermann had bought him a pair at a charity shop—a detail he kept to himself.

"Wow. The boys let you play?"

A stumble. "Yes. I was . . . determined."

"I suppose it's in your blood."

"How's that?"

"I bet you're used to fighting for every little thing."

After a pause, she said, "When I was a girl we had a houseboy named Henry Lum. He used to tend the coal and sleep on the floor in the basement. He never complained, but I felt guilty. One night I went down to check on him. Scared him half to death! He was terrified my parents would catch us down there and think the worst. I never went down there again."

When Mrs. Ostermann had shown Nelson how to tend the furnace, he had expected her to point to some bedding beside it. Instead, she gave him a room upstairs. Something of what he had felt for her then now extended itself to Tessa.

"My mother showed him how to fry bacon and eggs so she could sleep in. I remember how I used to come down to those wonderful smells and think that Henry was somehow my mother in disguise." She laughed. "Then came that horrible murder trial. Remember that? The Millards' houseboy? *I* would have swatted Mrs. Millard with a chair, too, if she had tried to cut off *my* ear. Wouldn't have thrown her body in the furnace, mind you, but I would have defended myself. Just unlucky to strike her dead. But my parents let poor Henry go. Suddenly scared of the help, like everyone else. Henry begged to stay but my parents had made up their minds. I cried, too, but it didn't help. Have you ever run across a boy by that name?"

"No."

"I suppose not. All those men in Chinatown. Lucky you. You have your pick."

It took a moment for Nelson to understand. When he did, he was taken aback. "I—I don't think about men."

She smiled, then gazed out into the night. "Gosh, isn't this beautiful?" she asked, knees drawn to her chest in wonder. As he traced her profile—the tip of her nose, the arc of her throat—he realized *this* was the wonder. That he should be here. With her. That they should be friends at all.

"What are you looking at?" she asked. She turned to

him. Under the play of starlight, her smile looked mischievous. "You can't fool me, Nellie. I know what you are."

His heart swelled painfully. For a long moment he didn't move. "What do you mean?"

"You don't have to pretend. I've seen the way you look at me. I know why you don't think about men. And those boots—they're a dead giveaway."

He swallowed bitterly. He had considered a new pair but the thought of crossing snow and ice in narrow heels had seemed even more incriminating. Now he wished he had thought differently. About everything.

"Don't worry. Your secret's safe with me."

He stared. "It is?"

"Of course. You shouldn't get kicked off the team for being . . . what you are."

He was baffled. Didn't she care that he was a boy? Was she that determined to win?

"Tessa?"

"Uh-huh."

His voice shook. "Tell me, what am I?"

"Do I have to say it?"

"Yes."

With a creak of leather, she rose from her chair and leaned over his, her hands atop the armrests, her face inches away, crowned by stars.

"You're what I am," she said. Then she kissed him.

———

Back in the passenger car, they clambered into bunks and looked across at each other until her green eyes winked out, leaving him alone with the train's eternal clacking. Outside, a silvery landscape slid past. At one point they crossed a truss arch bridge, so perilously high they might have been flying. Her lips had been cool and dry, testing at first, then more certain. When she pulled away, he thought he saw the ghostly afterimage of someone in the doorway. But no, that was impossible; it must have been a trick of light. Still, he had reason to be scared—and confused. After all, she hadn't really kissed *him*, had she? He knew women were up to wild and uproarious things these days, but kissing another girl? And wasn't it wrong for someone like her to take to someone like him? In certain cafés in Chinatown, white waitresses would go off with men for a dollar or two, and even Nelson thought them low for picking up dirty old Chinamen. As the train rumbled on, he tried to sleep but couldn't. The pillow was soft but the blanket surprisingly thin.

———

He fell asleep at first light. By the time he awoke, night had fallen again and they had reached Banff. Thanks to the carnival, the whole town was strung up with little white lights, as if Christmas went on forever in this part of the world. On the bus ride to the hotel, Edna flattened her palms against the window and said, "Look at that!"

"Stop the bus!" Tessa said.

In the center of town stood a castle of ice, complete with archways and turrets and battlements. It rose three stories, more if you counted the flags—Britain, France, Canada— and the whole thing glowed as if the ice were lit from within. They poured off the bus and into the castle and discovered a luminous, high-walled maze. "Last one out is a rotten egg!" Edna cried, which sent everyone scattering. Nelson ran ahead, feet slipping. His first turn led to a corridor. So did the next and the one after that. Then he ran into a dead end. He doubled back, ran faster. As he cut a blind corner he bumped into Tessa. They both reared up, arms raised, but couldn't avoid colliding. She let out a playful yelp.

"I'm lost," she said.

"Me too."

Tessa laughed, exposing the florid roof of her mouth, and the air between them slacked. Together they wandered the maze as voices around them called out and faded, until all that was left was the sound of their boots squeaking against hard-packed snow.

By the time they made it out, everyone else was gone.

"Maybe they're over there," Tessa said, pointing.

With long, loping strides, she crossed Banff Avenue and its median lined with carnival teepees and made for a steep side street. A chute ran down the center of the street and right through the castle. When the others couldn't be found, she said, "Come on, let's try the run!" Seizing a length of rope, she started dragging a toboggan up the sidewalk. At the top of the chute, Nelson sat down first, feet tucked under the board's curled lip. Tessa wrapped herself around him, and together they paddled with hands and feet until the board began to teeter. For a moment Nelson felt buoyant, suspended in midair. Then, with a visceral tug, they tipped over the edge and hurtled down the chute, bumping, rattling, verging on flight, both of them crying out, and Tessa clinging tightly.

After shooting through the castle and skidding to a halt, they fell upon each other, laughing. He slumped back, head in her lap, and she leaned forward, nose hovering.

A voice said, "There you are."

Mr. Lichtenhein loomed, his face dark. Nelson scrambled to his feet. Tessa got up slowly.

"Where is everybody?" she asked.

"On the bus," Mr. Lichtenhein said. "Waiting."

———

The Banff Springs Hotel was a chateau with heavy stonework and pitched green roofs, one of the famous Canadian Pacific Railway hotels that dotted the transcontinental line. In the dark-paneled lobby, a small army of bellhops shouldered their luggage and gear up the grand staircase. Libby and the sisters had been assigned to one room, the rest of the girls to another. Tessa walked in and sat on the bed by the window.

"Nellie and I will take this one."

Nelson's breath grew short. He grabbed his valise and hurried down the hall to the bathroom and slipped on a thick cotton nightgown and his mother's thin metal head-band. Then he took a deep breath and returned. The others had slipped into nightgowns, too, and the pale, ethereal, barefooted sight of them made him feel lightheaded. He lowered his eyes and climbed into bed.

"Nellie?" Tessa whispered when the lights went out, but he feigned sleep, his back turned, afraid of all the ways he might betray himself.

When he woke in the morning, he and Tessa were alone. She was looking down at him, head in one hand, her green eyes blue in the steel-gray light.

"How long have you been up?"

The corners of her mouth rose faintly. "A while."

A knock sounded. Nelson drew back.

"Rise and shine, girls," came Mr. Lichtenhein's unwel-come voice.

———

Mather's Rink was a perfect wooden rectangle on the bank of the Bow River. The day was crisp and clear, the ice glassy and hard. Swooshing around in warm-up, Nelson reveled in the open air, the miles of sky, and the ever-present view of craggy, snowcapped Cascade Mountain, which loomed over the whole town.

Their first game was against the Amazons. The rivals from Vancouver would play each other first, as would the rivals from Calgary, the Regents and the Patricias. That way, the championship game was assured of being an interprovincial battle. That morning, the Amazons looked especially loose, laughing and whooping and posing for pictures, the crowd two-deep on all sides. At one point, the lanky girl who had scored in Vancouver kissed her coach on the lips.

"Did you see that?" Nelson asked.

"What? Kit Carson and Guy Patrick? That's old news," Tessa said.

During warm-up, Nelson drew looks, even unabashed pointing. Over breakfast, Edna had read aloud from the carnival program: "'For glitz and glamour and a dash of novelty, come see the fair sex wield the twisted hickory!'" As she listed the teams, her face fell. "'—and the Vancouver Valkyries, featuring Nellie Woo, the World's First Asiatic Woman Hockeyist'?"

Mr. Lichtenhein sniffed. "They don't throw carnivals just for the sake of sport."

"I thought we were a team."

"We *are* a team," Tessa said. "And we're here. To play for the championship. That's the important thing."

The referee skated to center ice in a tweed suit and flat cap, and the teams lined up, wingers on either side of the center, the rover and defenders directly behind. The crowd leaned over the boards and pounded them raucously.

On the opening face-off, Tessa and Kit Carson waged a long battle for the puck, both of them blocking out, lifting each other's stick. When Tessa finally swatted the puck back to Nelson, Kit Carson bristled. Unlike Denman Arena, whose scoreboard and lights had made Nelson tight, Mather's Rink and its fringe of trees reminded him of Lost Lagoon, where he'd always felt carefree, and his first feint led to open ice, his first rush to a clear shot. Hockey teetered on that fine line between confidence and fear, and today he felt good. Tessa must have felt the same; they seemed in sync. Halfway through the first period, when she dropped a perfect pass in the Amazons' zone, Nelson cradled the puck on his blade and aimed for his favorite spot: top shelf, far side.

The crowd roared as he leaped into Tessa's arms.

Between periods, as they sat in one of the warming huts, a shed with benches along the walls and a wood-burning stove in the middle, their coach laid out a new strategy: now that they had the lead, they were going to slow the game down. With two hands, he mimed a hook, a slash.

"That's not our game," Tessa said, rising.

"It is now," Mr. Lichtenhein replied.

In the second period, Tessa kept skating hard, hunting for more goals, and Nelson did the same, flying up and down the ice, but the others relished the chance to bump, hack, and whack. *Ow! Hey! Watch it!* the Amazons cried, clutching their legs, shooting dirty looks. They kept turning to the referee, arms raised, but the man just shrugged.

The strategy was working.

In the third, both teams came out furiously, throwing shoulders, sticking out hips, and bodies kept falling to the ice. After getting rapped on the shins, Edna hobbled after her assailant and laid out a lumberman's chop. The other girl crumpled and stayed down for a long time and had to be helped off by teammates. The referee glowered at Edna and pointed her off the ice. Both teams would have to play one short.

When play resumed, Kit Carson took over the game. With more room to maneuver, she swooped around the Valkyries, unleashing shot after spring-loaded shot until one eventually eluded Libby. "Stick to the game plan," Mr. Lichtenhein barked, but the momentum had swung, and Kit Carson kept slashing to the net, past suddenly timid defenders who could only wave their sticks, and in time she scored again, a bullet to the glove side, and the Valkyries flagged.

As time ticked down, Thelma and one of the Amazons joined in one last foot race to the puck, which had lodged itself in a corner. Both of them skated madly, elbows in the air. When it looked like she would lose this final skirmish, too, Thelma knocked the other girl's skates out from under her, sending her feetfirst into the boards.

What Nelson heard before the harrowing cry was the dry snap of a stick. Only no stick was broken.

———

After officials converged upon the scene and the game was called and the fallen girl taken away on a stretcher, the Valkyries sat in their warming hut until the silence swelled to bursting.

"We didn't have to play that way," Tessa said.

"The game plan was working. Maybe you two"—the coach pointed at Tessa and Nelson—"should have followed it."

"We didn't have to play like . . . *men.*"

Mr. Lichtenhein drew up. "I'm surprised at you, Tessa. You of all people should know that hockey is hockey."

She made as if to say something but didn't. In fact, she didn't say anything else all day, not as the team stood in the cold watching the Regents beat the Patricias, not on the ride back to the hotel, the bus conspicuously theirs alone, and not as the team sat cheerlessly down to dinner in the dining room. It wasn't until the Amazons came trudging through that Tessa finally spoke: "How is she?"

Kit narrowed her eyes. "Her leg's broken."

"Good god. I'm sorry."

"Clara can hardly walk, either."

Thelma and Edna stared at their plates.

"Then how will you play tomorrow?"

Kit turned to Guy Patrick, who nodded grudgingly. "Guy talked to the officials," she said. "They're letting us find replacements. But they have to be from British Columbia. The final has to be interprovincial." She paused, letting the news sink in. "We'd like you to play for us, Tessa. And you, too, Nellie. You're the only ones who played clean."

"No!" Mr. Lichtenhein boomed, rising to his feet. The whole room turned.

Guy Patrick stepped forward, his blond hair swept back atop his high forehead. "This is about more than you and me, George."

"Is it? Would you feel the same if I were poaching your players?"

"Yes, if it meant beating Alberta."

"If you two play," Mr. Lichtenhein warned, eyeing them back and forth, "you'll be finding your own way home."

Tessa's eyes slivered. "You're a fine one, aren't you?" She rose from her seat and stalked off, and the Amazons followed suit. One by one the Valkyries pushed back their chairs, but when Nelson got up, Mr. Lichtenhein wagged his fork. "Sit down, Nellie. We need to talk."

Libby gave Nelson a rueful look, then left him to his fate. Mr. Lichtenhein set down his knife and fork, his mustache pearled with gravy. "You and Tessa have gotten mighty close. Thick as thieves, I'd say."

Nelson's jaw loosed.

"She has some kind of . . . influence over you, doesn't she? You can hardly be blamed, of course. She's a very influential girl. From a very influential family. Her father is a barrister. Do you know what that means? Let's just say her family might not be too happy to know whom she's been . . . consorting with."

Nelson blinked rapidly.

"Tell me something. Do you have a brother?"

"Pardon, sir?"

"A brother. Do you have one?"

"No, sir."

"Are you sure? I saw someone at a boys' tryout who looked a lot like you."

"I'm an only child."

Without warning, Mr. Lichtenhein reached across the table, took him by the chin, and turned his face from side to side, his fingers thick, coarse, vulgar. Nelson's eyes burned.

The man finally let go and dabbed his lips with a napkin. Then he threw the napkin down and rose to full height.

"Don't play."

————

Nelson returned to his room to find Thelma and Edna playing cards on the bed.

"Where's Tessa?"

Edna raised her eyes. "Why are you asking us?"

Sensing the chill, he backed out of the room and wandered the hotel, through vaulted, dimly lit passageways that made him feel deep underground. Eventually, he came to a glassed-in room filled with greenery and white wicker furniture. There he found Tessa taking in the dusky view of the valley beyond.

"I—I don't think we should play."

Her brows cinched. "You can't be serious."

"It's not really fair, is it? He brought us here to play for *him*. And he's paid for everything—"

"Don't be fooled, Nellie. Every team gets a share of the gate."

"But how will we get back?"

"Don't worry. My father will pay our way, if it comes to that."

He imagined the barrister and the barrister's wife catching sight of him at the station. "Won't your parents be upset if—"

"Who cares what my parents think?" she snapped. "All they think about is 'society'—and marrying me into it. Mother especially. I'm sick of it."

Her attitude surprised him. "My mother's dead."

She searched his face. "I'm sorry. And your father?"

"Gone, too. I live with my . . . uncle."

"What does he do?"

"He runs a laundry. *We* run a laundry."

Tessa nodded faintly, and Nelson was certain that everything had changed.

"What's going to happen to us?" he asked.

Tessa's eyes sharpened. "We're going to be together, Nellie. All the better if you don't have parents to stop you." She gripped him by the shoulders. "In Paris there's an art collector—she's a writer, too—and she lives with a woman and everyone knows, it's all out in the open. We don't have to be afraid. It's a whole new world out there."

Until that moment, he had thought of her as someone very different, perhaps impossibly different, but now he saw that they were in fact the same: neither wanted to be what the world expected.

"Okay," he said, "I'll play."

———

That night, after everyone had gone to bed, Thelma claiming a "doozy" of a headache, Nelson slipped down the hall and ran a bath. As he lay in the tub, water rising stingingly over his blackened shins, he looked at himself, at the part of himself that now seemed to stand between him and happiness. Could he go on pretending, maybe in Paris, or would he have to do something drastic? Those eunuchs of old, they'd had affairs with the concubines they guarded, so they must have still felt *something*. Could he go through life like that if it meant being with Tessa?

If he didn't entertain the thought for long, it was because he nursed a secret hope: that she might come to love him for who he was. That he might reveal himself one day, to her utter joy and amazement. It wasn't impossible to think. Didn't some part of her want a normal life? And wouldn't he still scandalize her parents, if that's what she was after?

Back in their room, he found Tessa lying in bed, seemingly out for the count, but as soon as he climbed in, she turned, drew close. He flinched.

"We can't. Not here."

"Just to say good night. Don't worry, they sleep like bears."

She pressed her lips to his, her breath milky and sweet, and he gave in to the dream, the lavish impossibility of it all, even though what he was doing amounted to a kind of theft. But just as guilt threatened to ruin the moment, he remembered what Sammy used to say whenever they stole onto streetcars or filched penny candy, trying to claw back a little of what the world had denied them: *It ain't stealin' if you're owed.*

———

Nelson woke to a ribbon of daylight stretched across the bed. Tessa was still asleep, so he studied her, lashes curled to alien length. He couldn't believe the sight he was waking to. That it might yet be his for the rest of his life. When Mrs. Ostermann had taken him in, he had also awoken to a new and beautiful life, there in her turreted house on leafy Nicola Street, but after only a few months she had taken ill and died. So even as he hoped for more, he pressed the morning into memory, afraid there would never be another.

He went down the hall and changed as the others slept. By the time he returned, Tessa was ready to go. "Don't be surprised if we run into Lichtenhein," she said, but they saw no sign of him in the lobby. "Guess he knows he can't stop us," she crowed, her shoulders relaxing.

On the bus, Kit said, "Here, you'll need these," and handed each of them what looked like a fresh stack of linen.

"What's the matter?" Tessa asked once the bus was in motion.

He hadn't thought about having to change. "Nothing. Just . . . nervous."

In the warming hut, he stood in a corner with his back

turned. He started by sliding off his cap, mournfully, as if facing a firing squad. Then he peeled off his sweater, first one arm, then the other before lifting the whole thing over his head, careful not to let his undershirt ride up. He had never felt so broad-shouldered, so criminally strong as he did in that moment, fumbling with his new sweater. When he finally got it on, he paused, took a breath. Now came the *hard* part. He unbuttoned his culottes and eased them to the floor, then rolled off his socks until all that remained were thin cotton bloomers. Then he did it all in reverse, one leg at a time, willing himself not to wobble or fall—all the harder for keeping his thighs pinched.

When everything was finally on, he turned, expecting the whole room to be stock-still and staring. But no one was paying him the least bit of mind.

———

Over the course of the morning the weather turned. An unruly mix of warm and cold air conspired to throw a blanket of fog over the entire valley, low to the ground like smoke from a brush fire. In warm-up, Nelson could hardly see the crowd, much less the trees or Cascade Mountain beyond. What was absolutely clear, though, was that the Regents, two-time defending Western Canada champions, were *good*. Not just good but big, a team of giantesses save for one who dashed around the ice like a scrappy little terrier. A gust blew through him and he shivered. He turned to

Tessa, hoping for assurance, but she was lost in thoughts of her own.

The teams skated to center ice.

The crowd roared.

Here it was. For all the marbles.

As soon as the puck dropped, the Regents attacked, a blur of green. They carried the puck deep into Amazon territory, and the newly formed squad struggled to get it out. It didn't help that visibility was next to zero and the crowd squarely behind the champs, who came in waves, streaking out of the fog like apparitions. Nelson felt cowed, in a fog of his own.

Then a break. With most of the Regents deep in the Amazons' zone, a drop pass jumped a stick at the blue line. Catching the last defender flat-footed, Nelson scooped up the puck and took off, nothing before him but a shrouded floe of ice. Down its length he raced for what seemed like miles, giantesses in pursuit, champing at his heels, but when their smudge of a goalie emerged from the fog, Nelson was still in the clear. As he cut across the goalmouth, the goalie flopped, pads stacked. He went to his backhand, dug his blade into the ice and pitchforked, hard. Rubber leaped into the air, up and over the goalie's pads.

Jubilation.

It was one of those goals that changes the whole complexion of a game. Suddenly the ice was level and play went back and forth, the Amazons plucky, resurgent, and urged on by their coach: "Don't sit back! Go for more!"

Just the opposite of Lichtenhein!

Now came the Amazons' turn to swarm. They kept the puck alive on offense, retrieving it time and again. Playing with Kit, Nelson felt her talent all the more: the beautiful stride, the feathery touch, the wicked wrister. He drew courage, and so did Tessa. The three of them found chemistry, a suddenly dangerous trio.

And then it happened: the dam broke. Kit scored on one of her patented shots and Tessa knocked home a lucky dribbler, and just like that, victory seemed assured. Western Canada champions! Nelson could hardly believe it. Who cared if it was a title in name only? For once he was going to win.

In the last few minutes, as the Regents grew more and more despondent, Nelson turned to Tessa. This time she saw him, and the look they exchanged was tender and knowing. This trip would mark them. Neither would ever be the same again.

That's when that little terrier of a girl reared up between them. "You ugly bastard," she said.

He had heard those words so often that they had no effect; he simply skated away. After a few strides, a stick appeared between his skates. It couldn't have taken more than a split second for the blade to rise and complete its arc, yet Nelson had time to note how strange a place that was for a blade to be, a moment before an explosion of pain made the world go dark.

He woke to a pain in his eyes, a blinding whiteness, then saw by degrees a white sheet, white bars at the foot of the bed, white walls and a white floor, and a jar full of cotton balls atop a white table. His whole body ached.

He lifted the sheet and then his paper-thin gown and found a patch of gauze between his legs. He peeled it back. What mattered most remained, but one of the organs below was gone, replaced by a grisly track of stitches.

It all came back to him: the game, the sweet nearness of victory, and something that hadn't struck him at the time, the word *bastard*. So the girl must have known, but how? Had Thelma or Edna heard something and told? Or had Lichtenhein shared whatever he knew or suspected? If the game had gone the Regents' way, maybe nothing would have come of his strange suspicions, but when the game went awry, there was only one way to keep the Amazons from winning. Whatever had made Lichtenhein keep what he knew to himself must have vanished as soon as Nelson switched sides. Was that what had happened?

From somewhere voices approached. Nelson closed his eyes.

"Is he up yet?"

Footsteps entered, retreated. "Not yet."

A man grunted. "Let me know as soon as he is."

There was no mistaking the voice of authority. How soon had a doctor made the discovery—rink, ambulance, hospital?—and told the police? Who would believe him now, that he just wanted to play hockey?

Through half-closed eyes, he surveyed the room. His hockey stick and valise were gone, but he saw his boots and his coat. When the hallway stilled, he eased himself out of bed and tiptoed to the window. One story up, minus a few feet of snow. He slipped on his boots and his coat and turned the latch to the double-hung window, then pulled on the small brass handle until it bit into his fingers, but the pane wouldn't budge. So he placed both hands at the top of the sash and pushed with his whole body, his effort checked by pain, a tearing sensation below. At last the pane gave way with a terrifying rattle. He froze, waiting for doctors and nurses and constables to charge into the room. When no one appeared, he turned his back to the window and put his hands behind him and raised himself onto the sill, cold air gushing all around him. Gingerly, he swung his legs out the window until he sat on the edge, feet dangling.

It was wholly unnatural not to make a sound as he fell. When he landed, pain erupted everywhere.

But he was alive.

———

He couldn't really say how he found his way to the station or how he knew which train was which or how he summoned the strength to pry open a boxcar. And he didn't really know how he managed to hang on for two whole days in jouncing darkness, parched, hungry, and shivering, except perhaps by clinging to fever dreams of Tessa. No doubt she knew the truth by now, and it must have come as a shock. But maybe it was for the best. By the time he went to see her at her father's house in the West End, full of velvety opulence, she would have already absorbed the worst of it. Yes, she would still be terribly aloof, and he would have to beg forgiveness, but at least she would finally see him for who he was, and maybe in the fullness of time they could start over, this time on sure ground.

When Terminal Station finally appeared in the gray light of morning, he felt he had been away from the city for years and resolved never to leave again.

The note he had left outside the laundry was still there, which he took to mean that Fong Man hadn't even come home. But the stove was lit and Fong Man was in the back room, sitting on his palliasse with his eyes closed.

"Where have you been?"

"Away."

Fong Man opened his eyes. "Who said you could close the laundry?"

Nelson limped toward his palliasse, which now seemed as princely as any hotel.

"I did."

"You little dead ghost!" In one motion Fong Man picked up his rosewood cane and brought it down across the back of Nelson's knees. Nelson buckled.

"Did you think I wouldn't see this? That no one would recognize you?" The old man rattled a copy of *The Daily*

World. "All my life I've fought to be a man, and now you—"
He finished the thought with a blow. Then another and
another.

———

He wasn't sure how long he had been unconscious, hours or
days, when he was roused by sounds in the night. He tried
to sit up but couldn't, his body stiff, unwilling. He heard the
shuffle of feet, then the door to the back room open. Light
fanned in and a figure appeared in the doorway. He was
relieved it was only Fong Man.

But no sooner had he let down his guard than others
began to appear in the room. Four by his count—backlit,
faces obscured. Here they were, then, the authorities. Not
until they forced him out of bed and wrenched his arms
behind his back did he realize they were all young and in
plainclothes. But he didn't struggle, not as his wrists were
bound, not even when some kind of sacking fell over his
head. He felt the cool of the laundry floor, then a deeper,
wetter cold outside. His shoulders were steered, his head
pushed down. A chassis bounced, and leather groaned.
Then came the cough of an engine and the first crackle of
motion. It was all so alive to him now, every surface, every
sound. As he was driven to who knew where—an empty
field, an abandoned mine—he realized he had expected
Tessa to keep what had happened a secret, out of shame

or disbelief, but maybe she hadn't and others were now taking umbrage. Or maybe the umbrage was hers. It made him sad to think so. Now he understood that the forces around her would win, and one day she would stand at the altar, eyes welling for reasons only she would know.

Frigid air blew through the open chassis. Raw as it was, it felt tremendous. It had been a hard life, a life of eating bitterness, but now he wanted it all again. The cold nights on the streets, the warm nights with his mother. His mother's presence now seemed near, as did the snap of capes, the quake and thunder of hooves. Yes, they were coming for him, the Valkyries, and he to the things he was owed.

The Nature of Things

A S THE TRAIN PULLED OUT OF SHANGHAI SOUTH STATION, Alice buried her face in her hands. The train had been late, and she and Frank had waited for over two hours, the platform swelling, restless. When the train finally arrived, they found themselves caught in the onrush of those scrambling for third class. At first, Frank had kept an arm around her, pushing as they went, but when a boy being dragged by his mother lost his grip and fell, Frank let go. When she looked back, he was roping off the crowd with outstretched arms to keep the boy from being trampled. "Don't stop, Alice! Get on the train!" Those were his parting words.

Two days earlier, on what became known as Black Saturday, Frank had been called to the hospital. According to both English and Chinese reports, the bombing of the Great World

Arcade had been an accident. After being clipped by Japanese warships on the river, a Chinese pilot had tried to lighten his payload on the grounds of the Shanghai Racecourse, only to fall hundreds of yards short. Incredibly, Chinese bombs had also fallen on the Bund, right on the corner of Nanking Road. All told, nearly two thousand dead, more injured. Alice had tethered herself to the radio, waiting for Frank to come home.

"You need to stay with my aunt and uncle," he said when he returned.

She would have gladly taken the next train to Wuhu, two hundred miles to the west, as he was urging, but she noticed the pronoun he used. "*I* should stay with them?"

"I can't leave. Not now."

"Frank, this is war."

"Exactly."

For weeks she had heard the insouciance of Shanghai-landers in public, the British especially, who discussed impending war as if betting on horses, or worse, aggrieved by the prospect of rain on a picnic. So she loved Frank, she really did, for caring. Nonetheless, she felt a flare of resentment. They had come to Shanghai for his sake. Everything they had ever done was for him. She wanted him to put her first for once.

"We have to think about the baby."

"Which is why you should go."

"I don't want to have this baby without you."

She only meant that she wanted him to deliver their child, but they both heard the implications.

"I'll be fine. Both sides respect the Concession. This is practically France."

"Then I'm staying, too."

Even as she said this, she felt the dark impulse. Yes, she was professing love, resolve, fear of separation, but she was also trying to saddle his conscience: if you stay, you'll endanger all three of us.

But he wouldn't give in. As always, his mind was made up. They argued to exhaustion, until she relented. If she couldn't save Frank, she had to save herself. And their child.

————

Frank and Alice Yeung had known each other all their lives, ever since they were urchins scrabbling over the one and only playground in Vancouver's Chinatown. They both went to Strathcona Elementary, then King Edward High School, where Frank had been something of a wonder boy. Once, using only household materials—screws, wire, tinfoil, Mason jars—and a neon sign transformer, he had built his own little Tesla coil and held her hand to it, closer and closer until a purple spark leaped from the ring to the tip of her finger. No one was surprised that he wanted to go to medical school, even though he couldn't be a doctor, not really, at least not in Canada. To join the Royal College of Physicians—or any professional society, for that matter— you had to be registered to vote, but in 1930 the Chinese didn't have the vote.

"I don't want to move to America," she had protested softly once, reluctant to leave her mother, her father, her three younger siblings.

"Don't worry, I'll find a way."

That was Frank for you, so certain he was special, that he alone would beat the odds. With no medical school in town, though, he had to go to Toronto. Whenever he was gone, she felt doubly aware of life, first as she lived through it, then through her missives to Frank. Every spring when he returned, her letters came back in their own leather duffel, like salmon home to spawn. But after six long, lonely years, when he finally came back for good, he couldn't find a job. Nothing had changed. No one would hire him.

At the end of that summer, as Alice worked on the seating plan for their reception, Frank announced that he had found work. Apparently some classmates, ashamed, had begged around, and someone knew someone who knew someone at Hôpital Sainte-Marie.

"Where's that?"

"Shanghai."

"Oh, Frank," she said, eyes dampening.

Their honeymoon began with a voyage aboard the *Empress of Japan*. As a gift, Frank's father, a merchant, sent them first class. By day they walked the decks, lost themselves in reading rooms, swam in the indoor pool; by night they dined on turtle consommé and roast leg of lamb and danced to "Goody Goody" and "A Fine Romance." At the end of ten days, after stops in Honolulu, Yokohama, and Kobe, they reached teeming, sprawling, magnificent Shanghai. They stayed at the Palace Hotel, right on the Bund, which might have been Europe if not for the rickshaws and sampans. They played tourist at places like Yuyuan Bazaar, where the little steamer buns were the best they'd ever had, and for one heady week she was glad they had come.

Then they moved to a terraced house in the French Concession, and Frank started his rounds. He put in long hours, longer than he had to, from love of work and a need to prove himself. Shanghai was a veritable army of foreign doctors, and he was foreign-but-not-foreign. On the days she waited for him to come home, for life to resume in his presence, she felt a reprise of their time apart, all those abject years of waiting in Vancouver. She made a point to venture out, only to encounter the city's underside. Once, on Avenue Joffre, she saw a woman curse a rickshaw driver in French, then slap him across the face with a set of wrist-length gloves. Another time, she came to a little park whose first rule, posted on a sign outside, was THE GARDENS ARE RESERVED FOR THE FOREIGN COMMUNITY. All of this made Shanghai feel painfully familiar.

After a long, bleak winter, she started getting sick in the mornings. Then in July, trouble came down from the north. One night, a Japanese company stationed near Peking set off on night maneuvers. When one of the soldiers failed to return, they traded shots with the Chinese around the Marco Polo Bridge. It turned out the missing soldier had gone to visit a brothel, but it hardly mattered now; the wheels of war had been greased. Back in 1931, after the Mukden Incident, Generalissimo Chiang had conceded Manchuria. It was too far away, and his army simply wasn't ready. Six years later, his dream of sixty well-trained and well-equipped divisions was still just that, a dream, even with help from the Germans, friendly for the moment, but all talk now was of taking on the Japanese, those "dwarf bandits." Frank assured Alice that any fighting would be far from Shanghai. Still, when the Japanese took Peking before the month was out, she was alarmed—and for good reason, it turned out. The open country of the north would have made cannon fodder of the Chinese Army. The Generalissimo had saved his troops for the only place they had a fighting chance: the alleyways of Shanghai.

———

Frank's uncle and aunt—*her* uncle and aunt, as she thought of them now—were all doting chatter, a blizzard of Mandarin, when they met her at the station in Wuhu. She had met them only once before in Shanghai, yet her uncle waved on tiptoe, glasses glinting, and her aunt looped an arm through hers as if they were sisters. In the car—a chauffeured Lincoln Zephyr, sleek as a beetle—they sat one to each side in the back seat and plied her with food, steamed bread as white as snow and hard-boiled eggs crazed with black tea and soy.

The Yeungs dealt in Chinese medicine. This explained the family fortune, a brother at either end of a trans-Pacific enterprise. Though Alice wanted nothing more than to be alone, she didn't protest when her in-laws took her to an apothecary filled with dark ring-pull drawers and jars of desiccated unknowns and showed her off to their employees.

It wasn't until bedtime that Alice was finally left to unpack. At the bottom of her suitcase, she found a cloth-bound book she didn't recognize, a stowaway. She turned to the title page:

LUCRETIUS

ON THE NATURE OF THINGS

(*DE RERUM NATURA*)

Translated by T. E. Wallace

MA, Fellow of Trinity College, Cambridge

She shouldn't have been surprised. Before they were married at First United, they had argued over a church wedding. For her parents, church was a salve for toiling ignobly in a distant country, her father for so many years in a cannery that his cutting hand was now a frozen claw. For Frank, though, church was just a way of aping respectability. He was no heathen; he didn't need to be saved. He was always looking for his own way and seemed to find it in a bookstore in the International Settlement. More than once in the past year, he had tried to describe *De rerum natura* with a wild-eyed air of discovery. Alice herself was a woman of no great piety. If she used to go to church in Vancouver, it was largely for her parents' sake. Even so, she couldn't abide the things Frank said. What did he mean there was no God? God was as plain to her as her very existence. Irritated anew, she put the book back and shut her suitcase. Out of habit, she got to her knees and prayed.

———

The next day she received the first of his telegrams. That was the deal, a telegram every day. To save on coding, his telegrams were short, sometimes just a single Chinese character: home. That was enough to let her breathe again.

At the end of the week, she walked to a nearby hotel, closeted herself in a booth, slipped in a bronze token, and sat under slatted light for a few timed minutes.

"How are you feeling?" he asked.

Despite the bitter concoctions her in-laws insisted she drink, she felt run down—and thirsty, always thirsty—but she didn't want to rouse the doctor in him. "Fine."

"Got our first from the front lines."

She knew from XGOA, the government radio station in Nanking, that the Chinese had launched a massive assault on the Japanese Marine Headquarters in Hongkou.

"And?"

From the silence, she could tell it had been worse than he'd imagined.

"I thought the nurses were brave."

Not for the first time, she wondered if he didn't feel

something for one of the nurses. Under the wingspan of their wimples, the sisters could be startlingly beautiful. She had hoped her absence would tug at him, bring him to her sooner rather than later, but now she sensed some still greater devotion being forged in the crucible of the operating room.

If she were still in Shanghai, they would have been strolling arm in arm to Avenue Joffre for *zakuski*, little plates of smoked salmon, salted herring, pickled tomatoes, and the like, which went down well with warming shots of vodka, especially in winter. She could have said something affectionate like, "I miss eating at Tkachenko." Instead, she complained that Wuhu was provincial: no Little Moscow here. Before she could finish, a woman came on to tell them their time was up. Now was the moment to soften, to say something effusive, but all she managed was "Bye, dear. Talk to you next week."

———

At first there were hopes the war would be short. The goal was to drive the enemy out in one fell swoop. In the Japanese stronghold of Yangshupu downtown, where crossroads were staunchly defended by sandbag trenches, gun nests, and brambles of barbed wire, the Chinese managed, despite a lack of cover, to claw all the way down to Broadway, the last street before the river, but were finally stopped by the high walls of the wharf. The Japanese, nearly driven into the sea, held out long enough for reinforcements to arrive.

No, the war would not be short.

Incensed that China was putting up a fight, the Japanese bombed the city. Air-raid sirens became a daily, sometimes hourly occurrence. If Alice could sleep at night, it was only because she knew the French Concession went largely unscathed; only the Chinese districts lay in smoldering ruin. Still, she kept urging Frank to leave.

But he kept saying, "Might be safer now to stay put."

He had a point. Even South Station had been bombed, much to her disbelief. Women and children mostly, trying to flee as she had. But the soundness of his logic only made her angry. What he should have wanted above all else was to come to her. To them.

Once, a fellow doctor had tried to take Frank to the Shanghai Club, famed for its forty-foot-long bar where patrons sat in order of rank, taipans at the end with the best view of the Bund, but nowhere along its length was there a place for someone like him. "He's a doctor! He's Canadian!" his colleague had argued, to no avail; Frank was turned away and came home burning. His staying behind in Shanghai had something to do with being Chinese, which almost made her sympathetic. But it seemed like foolish pride to stick it out at any cost.

———

A month passed and her belly grew. She found herself capsized in bed, crab-walking in and out of chairs. The fitful limbs that stretched her belly made her think of an insect trapped in spider's silk, so she started calling the baby "Bug." She tried to entice Frank to leave with details of what he was missing—"You need to see this. It's really amazing"—and those were the moments when he seemed closest to coming.

Alice was surprised that in her state her body keened for Frank's. Every summer when he came back from Toronto, they would frequent the pool at Kitsilano Beach—the largest saltwater pool in the world. They weren't barred from entering, but they got their share of looks. Nonetheless, Frank always insisted on going. Not only that, he would make a point to swim the pool's length, all two hundred yards, in just a few breaths, then rise from the pool like Johnny Weissmuller himself, slicking his hair back with both hands. Sometimes, after stealing kisses all day, he would whisper, "I can't wait anymore," but despite being drunk from too much sun and feeling him through his woolen bathing shorts, she always insisted on waiting. Now those summers seemed like lost time.

———

September dragged into October. With each passing week, Frank seemed to grow more morose. Their weekly phone conversations were blighted by ever longer stretches of silence, precious, expensive seconds they couldn't afford to fritter away. "What's the matter, Frank?" she would ask, trying to bring him back, but she knew: the carnage was taking its toll. She asked Frank's uncle to speak to his brother and wrote to her parents asking the same. If Frank wouldn't leave as a husband and father, maybe he would leave as a son.

In early November, an unexpected landing at Hangzhou Bay, twenty miles from Shanghai. For weeks, the Japanese had been pushing down from the north from the Yangtze River; now they were also coming from the south. The objective was clear: outflank the city. The pincer was poised. Frank had to get out.

"Sister Marguerite thinks I should leave."

"Don't *you* think you should leave?"

Only the slightest pause before he said wearily, "Yes, it's time."

Alice soared. "Thank God."

For some reason the line went cold. Strange that he should seem low at the prospect of reunion. "What's the matter, darling? You seem blue."

At first he couldn't say. Then in a faltering voice: "I wanted to win. I wanted to beat the damn Japs."

———

Alice discovered newfound energy for her daily circuit around Mirror Lake, over the bridges and under the willows for a good half mile. "Daddy's coming, Bug, Daddy's coming," she would coo, cradling her belly. She wished Frank were only a train ride away, but rail was still too dangerous, so his plan was to catch a ride to Lake Tai and cross by boat, then hitch a ride or walk the rest of the way. From the west side of the lake, Wuhu was only a hundred miles.

Only three days after Frank set off, Shanghai fell, more quickly than expected, but Alice felt triumphant: he had made it out in time. All that was left was to conquer whatever distance remained. Every day she did the math, the number of miles he must have been traveling. The hardest part was no longer receiving telegrams: after a steady diet, it was painful to go without, but Frank had warned her not to expect them.

Four, five, six days passed. Each one brought rising hopes in the morning, creeping doubts at night. After a week she gave in to dread and called the hospital. With the indubitability of a head nurse, Sister Marguerite said she had last seen Frank five days ago. In fact, it was in the log for that day.

"Was there an emergency?" Alice asked.

"My dear," Sister Marguerite replied, "it's all an emergency."

Two days. Frank had stayed two more days without telling her. At first, in her confusion, she felt relieved. The hands of time whirled back a full forty-eight hours, making it more likely that he was still en route. Then darker thoughts invaded. What could possibly have kept him and why didn't he say? Suddenly her husband seemed someone wholly unknown to her. More painful still was the possibility, now distinct, that he'd been caught up in the chaotic Chinese retreat. With the enemy in pursuit, the troops had broken rank. At Lake Tai, it was every man for himself. In the struggle for passage, young and old alike got pushed under. She had thought Frank had escaped all that. Now all she could picture was him stupidly saving others before saving himself.

Every day from dawn till dusk, she sat outside, scanning the street, waiting for the first glimpse, the ecstatic moment, but it never came. Another week passed without any sign. By this point the Japanese had started marching toward Nanking. She had thought that the war would end with the fall of Shanghai, but the Japanese were not only pressing on but taking their pound of flesh. Throughout the countryside, villages were being torched. When she heard that men were being bound in groups, doused with gasoline, and set ablaze, she had to steady herself. In hindsight, it was obvious that Frank should have stayed put. After the city fell, thousands stretched their arms through the iron fence of the French Concession, so many they had to be held off with tanks. Everyone desperate to get in, and she had made him get out. In the small hours of night, Alice would curse herself, then Frank, then curse herself for cursing him. At unbidden moments, she fell to her knees and bartered with God. Sometimes she prayed that it was all an elaborate ruse, that a letter would soon explain how he had taken a ship to France with one of the sisters, now defrocked. Anything to know he was still alive.

———

The army kept falling back. The so-called Chinese Hindenburg Line was supposed to hold out for six months; it fell in two weeks. The Generalissimo took to the airwaves to announce that the government was moving to Chungking. That's when her uncle released his employees. The Japanese were not only closing in on Nanking but also making a break for Wuhu to cut off any retreat. Everyone had to leave.

"We have a family compound upriver," her uncle explained.

"What about Frank?" Alice blurted.

He touched a pensive hand to his glasses. "You two go first. I'll wait another day."

Her aunt made as if to speak but checked herself. It wasn't for her to object; it was for Alice to refuse. But she couldn't bring herself to pull up the lifeline.

When she went to pack, she found it again, the book Frank had given her, rearing up like an apparition. She ran a hand down its grainy cloth cover and pressed her nose to the open pages, inhaling the scent of paper and glue. Then she filled her suitcase and laid the book on top.

At dusk they made their way down to the Clearwater

River, less a river than a turbid, slow-moving stream. At the sight of the rickety-looking skiff, Alice wavered, afraid it would tip under her weight. But with help from her aunt aboard and her uncle ashore, she managed to sidle in. The skiff swayed, then steadied.

"See you soon!" her uncle cried, too brightly.

A young ferryman punted them upriver. For a while the only sounds were the drip and plash of his pole, but after darkness fell the sounds were obscured by a drone. At first it sounded like bees in a glade; then it took on a whirring mechanical edge. Sure enough, a constellation of black stars slid fiendishly across the sky. Then came whistling, flashes, thunderous claps. Downriver, fireballs ripped through the dark. Alice looked away, stricken by guilt, but her aunt was resolute: "He'll be fine. He knows what to do."

At first light, her aunt pounded on the gate of the family compound. *"Lao Zhang! Kuai dian kaimen!"* she shouted. Moments later, a wizened man appeared at the door and led them through the inner gate. The compound was a quadrangle with mulberry trees in the courtyard. After a sleepless night, Alice collapsed in one of the side rooms.

In the afternoon, she went back down to the river to look for her uncle. She brought Frank's book as a kind of talisman, but when the day stalled, she started leafing through it. The book began with an invocation of Venus: *Mother of Rome, delight of Gods and men . . .* When the first stanzas proved elusive, she riffled ahead until she saw a passage underlined in pencil:

Consider sunbeams. When the sun's rays let in
Pass through the darkness of a shuttered room,
You will see a multitude of tiny bodies
All mingling in a multitude of ways
Inside the sunbeam, moving in the void,
Seeming to be engaged in endless strife,
Battle, and warfare, troop attacking troop,
And never a respite, harried constantly,
With meetings and with partings everywhere.

The commonplace of dust. What did this mean and why did Frank care? He never mentioned giving her the book, never asked if she'd read it, but now his markings seemed to speak, to hold the key to why he had stayed. Her last glimpse of Frank had not been of him hovering over the boy and holding back the crowd at South Station. Instead, it came after the platform had thinned, as the train began to creak, when Frank ran up to her car and leaped to kiss her window, which startled her and made her snort. All the way to Wuhu, she had studied the smear of his lips, wishing she could reach through the glass and somehow preserve that scintilla of him. That's how she felt now, studying his markings, that Frank was near yet unreachable.

Intermittent traffic on the river. Sampans laden with bundles, children, chicken coops. But no sign of anyone she knew.

———

In the morning she awoke to commotion in the courtyard. From her bed she heard a man's voice—her uncle's— describing how he had cowered all night, waiting for the bombs to stop. He would have gotten here sooner if not for the army commandeering everything.

As soon as she opened her door, he said, "I left word with the neighbors. Frank will know where to go."

She had hoped Frank would be here too. Still, she was buoyed by the sight of her uncle. "He's coming. I feel it," she said.

Far from dashing her hopes, her uncle bolstered them: on his trip upriver, he'd heard that a Chinese general had disguised himself as a peasant in order to evade the Japanese. Maybe Frank had done something like that, she thought. Or maybe he had sprained his knee or twisted an ankle and knew better than to push it. Maybe he was holed up somewhere, nursing himself, biding his time. Anything was possible.

All day, she sat on the bank of the river, half-hidden in sawgrass. Again, she brought Frank's book, and when time dragged she studied his markings. Many converged around the idea that the universe was made of atoms—indivisible, indestructible. That much she could accept. But no sooner did she start to nod along than she found herself unsettled. *So from the body if mind and spirit be withdrawn, / Total collapse of all must follow* . . . The passage went on in that vein, and despite the prettified language, she sensed its meaning, and it troubled her, she who had grown up not only in the Church but in Chinatown, with all its talk of ghosts. One morning aboard the *Empress of Japan*, Alice had run into two elders from Chinatown. Both were pressing shabby hats to their heads to keep them from blowing away, and one had a face so mottled with age it might have been splattered with ink. Both were traveling steerage but had somehow managed to find her. "*Gongxi! Gongxi!*" they cried, pleased that the "little dumpling" of Chinatown had finally gotten married. Now here were men who knew the ravages of time and distance, who had seen their wives only a few times in decades, on those rare occasions when they went back to China. Men for whom a mere six years would have been a mercy. Most of these men were now too poor or too ashamed of their poverty to move back to China, but the Great Depression came bearing an unexpected gift: a ticket home in exchange for the promise never to come back, which was cheaper for the powers that be than offering people relief. And this made the old men happy. They were going home to die. Their ghosts wouldn't be doomed to wander Gold Mountain forever.

What was Frank trying to say through the book? That these men were wrong? That it didn't matter where they died? It bothered her, his skepticism, and the feeling that he was trying to disabuse her of something.

She set the book down and gazed at the river, where traffic today was heavier. What she saw mostly were ragged bands of soldiers, rifles in hand, cigarettes dangling. At one point, a young, hungry-looking soldier spied her on the bank—alone, supine, bursting with life—and kept his eyes fixed as his skiff puddled past. He stared with such intent that she was sure he would leap off the skiff and splash toward her, drenching himself as he went. By the time he cleared the bend, her heart was surging painfully. Not just from fear but also the knowledge that she hadn't looked away.

In her guilt, she recalled something Frank had told her, that despite once being widely read, *De rerum natura* virtually disappeared during the Middle Ages until a rare medieval copy was found in a monastery during the Renaissance. That, she decided, was what Frank was really trying to say, that he, too, would slip through the bottleneck. That he and he alone would come to her.

———

It took a day for Alice to realize they should have been on the move, too, that her in-laws were tarrying for her sake, letting her keep vigil. "If we have to leave . . ." she said in the morning, and her in-laws nodded, relieved.

As her uncle gathered food, she helped her aunt sew money into the lining of their clothes. Before they could finish, however, the family servant, Old Chang, burst through the inner gate and locked it frantically behind him. *"Riben ren laile!"* he gasped. "Are you sure?" her uncle asked. The old man nodded. "White bandannas," he said, tying an imaginary one around his head. "On the crest of the hill."

Her uncle's brow buckled. He looked at Alice, at her distension, and said, "It's too late to run. We have to hide."

"Where?" his wife asked.

Her uncle surveyed the house in his mind, then strode to the very back, to a long, narrow, dimly lit room with a marble counter along its length, atop which sat two candles, a platter of oranges, a censer full of charred stalks, and dozens of red and gold funeral plaques, rising like buildings in a model city. The altar room.

Below the counter was a cabinet with a small door. Her uncle slid it open.

Her aunt peered. "Are you sure?"

"We have no choice."

Her aunt lowered herself to the floor. Out of modesty, she sat down and backed in, so it seemed she was not so much entering as being swallowed whole. "Are you all right?" her uncle asked once she was in. "Yes, yes," she replied impatiently, her voice already cavernous. Alice sat down, helped by her uncle and Old Chang, the stone floor plungingly cold. After walking her haunches over the lip of the door, she slid back, hands pocked with grit. She should have loosed her bun, which would have given her poor neck an extra inch of space. As it was, she sat with her face nearly pressed to the sudden monstrosity of her belly.

"After I get in," her uncle instructed Old Chang, "put some stools in front of the altar. Then unlock the gates. If they can't get in, they'll burn the house down. Open some drawers, make it look like we've left in a hurry. Then climb onto the roof and stay out of sight. Don't come down till they're gone. Can you manage that?" Alice heard no reply, only what sounded like a clap on the back, and she pictured a lifetime of fealty, Old Chang carrying a boy on his shoulders. Then her uncle got in and the world went dark.

The slap and shuffle of Old Chang's slippers, retreating, returning, retreating again. Stools scraped, drawers whinnied, and then the house fell silent. Alice would have felt safer in total darkness, her body dematerialized, but a gap between two panels let in a spray of light, enough to prove that she was still there. If she angled her head just so, she could see out, the breach sharpening the room like a lens, and this made her fear the opposite, that someone might see in, catch her eyes glinting in darkness. So she closed them and in that more complete darkness wondered how her life had come to this.

If her ghost were left to wander here, would it feel lost or at home?

A pounding at the gate. Belligerent shouts, muffled, remote, then ringingly clear. Footsteps in the house, dozens of sets, it seemed, all scurrying toward them. The splintering of wood, the bursting tinkle of china, and raucous laughter, all strangely amplified by the roaring in her ears.

In no time, footsteps were outside the altar room door, where they slowed, quieted. With what seemed like caution, unseen figures entered. Had they heard something? Was one already holding a finger to his lips and pointing? Out of sheer terror, Alice opened her eyes. Through the breach, she glimpsed camel-toed shoes, tightly wrapped puttees, and the dull gleam of a bayonet.

She prayed, hard.

As if in answer, the soldiers muttered and left. Alice couldn't tell how long she was forced to stay there, tensed in silence, waiting for the soldiers to finish ransacking the house, but by the time Old Chang came padding back, every muscle in her body yowled for release. There was no more blood in her legs. She could hardly stand. But she was alive.

"They were afraid," her uncle said. "They have no mercy for the living, but they still respect the dead."

If not God, then ghosts. Someone had saved them.

Suddenly Alice was in flight. She ran to her room and tore through the clothes that now lined the floor. And there it was, still, her book.

———

"We can't stay," Old Chang said. "More are coming to spend the night. I heard them."

Warm beds. Provisions. Of course they would be back. But the four of them couldn't exactly run, not with the enemy everywhere. Better to let the first wave pass and take their chances later.

In a copse beyond the house was a wooden shed, her uncle said. They could spend the night there. As soon as they gathered themselves, they dared the few hundred yards to the woods, the men lugging a ladder between them. When they came to the old battered shed and its makeshift boards, Old Chang clambered onto the roof and Alice was made to follow. The ladder was then raised and thrust down through the skylight, and she climbed down. Only then did she understand the elaborate entrance: the shed was full of rice. She stifled laughter, sinking into the unexpected dune.

The ladder retracted and reappeared until all of them were safely in. There on the rice, they made little beds for themselves, Alice relieved for something reasonably solid against the small of her back. Within the hour, the coughing of engines, followed by drunken revelry long into the night.

———

Sometime in the night, Alice awoke from a dream she instantly forgot. The others were still asleep, her in-laws huddled together for warmth, Old Chang off in a corner, and the shed unexpectedly bright. The gloaming that had fizzled in like a mist was now a clear shaft of moonlight, teeming, undulant, alive. Motes of dust they must have kicked up themselves were still floating, spinning, swirling through the air. She watched them flit and dodge, dance and collide, coming together and breaking apart *in endless motion through the mighty void.* She looked on with something like awe.

———

Long into the morning, the four of them stayed put until every last engine had rumbled away. Then they ventured out, blinded, dazed. As they set off, Alice slowed, letting the others walk ahead. When she felt safely behind, she turned and looked back.

Somehow she wasn't surprised to see Frank at the edge of the copse. Nor was she surprised that he hadn't called out. There he stood in his wedding suit, looking as gentle, handsome, and proud, as untarnished by life as the day they were married, and she raised an arm, her heart smote by joy. Joy that flamed into the air, filling the woods, the universe. Then Frank did something strange. With lips pursed, he bent his knees and leaped into the air, and all that heat went cold.

In that moment there were any number of things she didn't know. For instance, that she would survive the day. That the four of them would make their way to the banks of the Yangtze River and fight the spray of water cannons, trying to board a British steamer. That Old Chang would slip and fall in the chaos and never be seen again. She didn't know that she would lie in an iron hold for five days without so much as matting until they reached Wuhan, or that from there they would go on another two hundred miles by train to Changsha, where with ether and an episiotomy she would give birth to a son at the hands of a stranger. Neither did she know that by the time they reached Hong Kong the whole world would be descended into madness, nor that, one month after she set sail for home, the Japanese would take on the British, too. She didn't know that China would eventually win, or that after the war she would vote for the first time, or that one day her only grandchild, a boy, would play soccer on King's College Circle and walk in cap and gown through Convocation Hall in Toronto, just like his grandfather. She didn't know that one day she would see her great-grandchildren through a magic portal she could hold in her hands, and she didn't know that in the end her ashes would be scattered over the Huangpu River, which curled like a hairpin through the heart of Shanghai, the last place she had been truly happy, though life would not be without happiness, as far as happiness went.

And she didn't know if she believed in God or the afterlife. All she knew, what she finally came to accept, was that the sweet, inimitable assemblage of atoms that was Frank Yeung was no more. And indeed, when she looked again, he was gone.

The Night of Broken Glass

BEFORE THE WAR, WHEN WE LIVED IN VIENNA, I MADE A habit of greeting my father when he came home from work. The Steiner School let out at three o'clock, which gave me time to walk the good half-mile from the Graben in the First District to our town house in the Third, change out of my uniform, ask the cook for something to eat, and read a Sanmao or Tintin comic, all before my father returned. My reward for standing at the door was usually little more than a nod or a grunt of approval. Still, I met him every day because I loved and respected him and felt it my duty.

One day my father came home in his flannel suit, topcoat, and snap-brim fedora, his briefcase and unused umbrella in hand. The day had been fair, with nothing to trouble my walk home, but my father stepped through the door with a deep-furrowed look. Now that the world was topsy-turvy, he often returned from the legation—or rather, since March, the Chinese Consulate General of the German province of Ostmark—with a harried expression, but that day his face was grave, almost ashen, and my greeting went unacknowledged. Reflexively, he asked our manservant for the day's briefing. With eyes downcast, Old Chao reported that the American had visited again. My father remained calm, but the hat traveling from his hand to Old Chao's hitched in mid-air. The American, whom I had never met, was an old high school classmate of my mother's, apparently in Europe on business. When my father had proposed dinner, my mother had said, "He's not so important. Not like one of your dignitaries," in a tone that left me unsure who was being slighted. So I was surprised, as my father must have been, that the man had come calling for the second time that week.

Over dinner my parents said little. Curiously, my mother made no mention of her friend, and my father did not deign to ask. He did, however, make a show of reading the paper. At the end of the meal, in an overflow of irritation, my mother criticized the cook for the profiteroles. Too dense, she said, and too soggy. The cook, a hobbled old woman they had brought with them from China, listened with head bowed before backing out of the room.

My father set down his paper with a crackle. "Why do you ask her to make things she doesn't know how to make?"

"Because I want to eat them."

"But there's no need to scold."

My mother smiled, as if at a child's fanciful idea. "You coddle them."

"No, I consider them."

My mother lifted her eyes to the ceiling, then left the room, and my father shook his head, trying to understand how, with so much going on in the world, his wife could possibly fret over profiteroles, or as she put it in her American way, cream puffs.

———

I met my mother for the first time when I was six. I say "mother" because that was what I was expected to call her, and did, though in fact she was my stepmother. My real mother died of tuberculosis when I was five. A year later my father came home with a new wife. He had been studying international law in Chicago despite already having a Ph.D. in political economics from the University of Munich. While he was gone I received a series of brightly colored linen postcards of the World's Fair: the Hall of Science, the Avenue of Flags, the iron lattice towers of the Sky Ride. The theme of the fair was "A Century of Progress." That's where my father met Grace.

It was a windless, thick-aired summer day in Changsha when a motorcar saddled with steamer trunks pulled up in front of our house and a woman in a white blouse, wide-legged trousers, and large sunglasses climbed out. She was beautiful, which made me sad for my mother and scornful of my father, and she looked too fair to be Chinese. As it turned out, she was half Chinese, born of a Chinese father and a German American mother. That, along with her clothes and her beauty, made her unlike any woman I had ever seen.

My father had secured a large two-story house on the outskirts of town and staffed it with half a dozen servants, all in an effort to make his new wife comfortable, but as soon as they arrived he was stricken by all he had not foreseen. The house had no running water, and Grace refused to use the privy, which had no seat and emitted at that time of year an audible drone. After pleading with Grace in hushed tones, my father ordered Old Chao into town for a portable commode, a trip of at least three hours. For the rest of the afternoon my new mother paced the courtyard, smoking one Lucky after another, which made her seem feral and caged.

If I kept my distance that day and in the first appraising weeks to come, it was because she didn't speak a word of Chinese and I didn't yet speak English. My father hired a tutor, but Grace learned to say only a few innocent things, and only in the toneless way of foreigners. Our only hope, then, was that I learn English, which I did soon enough, through sheer exposure. Grace spoke in torrents and paused only to teach me phrases like *hot diggity dog!* and *Now you're on the trolley!* which, when repeated by me, elicited barking laughter from her.

Needless to say, Grace was unhappy in China. Though my father had no particular desire to leave, he began to eye the foreign service. When the governor for whom he worked recommended the post of first secretary in the Chinese legation in Austria, my father accepted for Grace's sake. We arrived in Vienna in June of my tenth year, after a three-week voyage on the *Conte Verde* via Saigon, Singapore, Madras, Bombay, Aden, and Port Said. The city was glorious with summer, and everywhere open-air orchestras paid homage to the old masters, which made our lives seem set to music. Many nights, my parents put on tails and gown and went to balls and receptions, living at last the life they were meant to live.

At first everything did seem better, but it wasn't long before Grace again felt stranded. She could no more distinguish *der, die,* and *das* than she could first and second tones. Then, in the spring, German troops goose-stepped through the Ringstrasse, just blocks away from our town house. The crowds that greeted them were lusty, adoring, as was I, my schoolboy fantasies of soldiers and guns come to life. My father did not raise his arm but he didn't stop me from raising mine. That night, in a scene that would soon become commonplace, hoodlums took to the streets, smashing the windows of certain homes and shops. Thereafter, walking to and from school, I passed storefronts marked *Jude* and *Nicht arisches Geschaeft* and blocked by baby-faced men in jackboots and flared helmets. As a visible foreigner and part of the diplomatic corps, my father felt undeterred and often went into these stores despite the piercing glares— and once, despite an arm held stiffly against his chest. For my mother, annexation was yet another rung of descent in a private tragedy. She chided my father for bringing her to a Nazi-occupied country. His answer: "Better the Germans than the Japanese."

At the end of October, thousands of Polish-born Jews were rounded up and sent back to Poland. When a seventeen-year-old boy learned that his family was among those languishing at the border, unwanted by either side, he walked into the German Embassy in Paris and pumped five bullets into the viscera of a minor German diplomat, and two days later, Ernst vom Rath died of his wounds. The seething of the Germans, in check so long as their countryman clung to life, would now be unleashed. This was what my father knew when he came home that afternoon.

————

I have very little memory of the rest of that night. I have a vague recollection of waking to the sound of breaking glass, but this may be a superimposition of what I learned afterward. Even if memory can be trusted, I don't recall anything else, which means I must have simply gone back to sleep.

By the time I awoke, my father had already left and made clear to Old Chao that I was not to go to school—or to leave the house, for that matter. When I asked why, Old Chao wouldn't say. Miserable with curiosity, I slipped out the door as soon as I found myself alone. We lived on Beethovenplatz, a square near the Stadtpark whose centerpiece was a seated bronze statue of the man himself, his expression eternally gloomy. There I was met by the air of something charred and ashes wafting like blackened snow, but it wasn't until I turned onto the Ring that I realized something was terribly wrong. It looked as though a violent storm had blown through in the night. Every other storefront was shattered and their wares strewn about, as if contents under pressure had exploded, and everywhere shards of glass lay glinting in the morning light. Amid the wreckage, women and children rummaged, pocketing whatever they pleased. At one point I passed a bookshop. An elderly man in a derby stood atop a heap of books on the sidewalk, picking through those that hadn't been scorched or torn. When he saw me, he reddened with shame. Then he drew up indignantly, remembering his place—and mine. I hurried on. Eventually I came upon an odd scene: a group of what looked like patients standing in a crude circle in the middle of the street, white-haired and rheumy-eyed and still in their nightclothes, as if they had just come from bed. Despite the apparent difficulty, they were made to perform calisthenics—slow-moving knee bends, jumping jacks—by men in brown shirts, black ties, and red armbands. All the while, boys my age in replica uniforms circled about maniacally, pointing and shouting and laughing, and this more than anything struck me with fear.

I ran home.

———

Years later my father described how quotidian the city had seemed that morning, everything up and running, as if nothing of consequence had happened. He was able to catch his usual tram, eager to get to where he was needed most. Earlier that fall, a line had begun to appear every day outside the consulate. Word had spread through cafés and synagogues: the consul general of China signed visas for those who asked. But that day of all days, to my father's surprise, there wasn't a single person outside.

"Hasn't anyone come?" he asked Zhou, the vice-consul, who lived upstairs.

"Some were here earlier, but they were . . . taken away."

"Why didn't you stop it?"

Zhou looked stricken. "How?"

My father sighed. He imagined himself dashing out, throwing up a diplomatic shield, but perhaps he, too, would have watched from the safety of his second-floor window.

That morning's papers were scant. According to one, last night's events had not disturbed "the hair of a single Jew." But over the course of the morning, news came in by cable, telephone, telex: dozens dead; countless terrorized; and everywhere, mass roundups.

In the afternoon, a black Buick Eight with small Chinese flags flapping on either side of the hood appeared in front of the consulate, and from it emerged the only person who could be in possession of such a car: Chen Chieh, the Chinese ambassador. Or rather the ambassador-designate; Hitler had so far refused to let him present his credentials. Germany's only interest in the Far East was containing the Russians, a task for which Japan now seemed best suited.

Nonetheless, when the man entered, my father extended him full diplomatic courtesy: "Your Excellency."

Chen appeared pleased as he took off his coat and hat and handed them to Zhou, who left the room sheepishly. "I heard that you were a smart man, Consul General Ho. You haven't disappointed."

"You should have told us you were coming. We would have made preparations."

Chen raised a hand. "No need to stand on ceremony."

He took a seat across from my father, chin short, earlobes long, and hairline receded to the top of his head like a Manchu. He wore a three-piece suit and thick, round glasses, and he spoke in the haughty Shanghainese way, without nasal inflection. My father waited for him to begin. Instead, Chen picked up the leather-bound copy of the Luther Bible on my father's desk. My father had grown up attending the boys' school on the campus of the Norwegian Lutheran Mission in Changsha. That's where he learned both English and German. It irked him that the ambassador had palmed the Book so blithely.

"You're a believer, then."

When my father said nothing, Chen's smile crimped, faded. He set the book down.

"I understand you've been signing visas for . . . those in need."

"Yes, that's right."

Chen tented his fingers and nodded. "You're entirely in the right, of course. But perhaps we ought to be more cautious. We know how the Germans feel. Especially now. We don't want to risk upsetting them further."

My father sat upright. "But we have our orders."

The ambassador fleered. "We know the motives of the Executive Yuan."

It was true that by offering passage to Jews the government hoped to raise funds for the war of resistance against Japan. It was also true that my father wanted in some way to join that war, haunted as he was by the carnage in China, Nanking especially, and his guilt that he was safely beyond its reach. But these were hardly his only motives.

"Where are they supposed to go?" my father asked. "Who will take them?"

"They may go to China if they wish, but they won't need visas. Shanghai is an open port. There's no passport control under the Japanese."

"But they need proof of passage in order to leave Austria—Ostmark."

"A steamship ticket is sufficient."

"A visa is better."

"That may be so, but Germany is our ally. We don't want to damage our warm relations."

My father had once had great affection for Germany, but it was Germany that had advised Generalissimo Chiang to abandon Nanking.

"Perhaps we should consult the vice-minister."

"You needn't worry about that," Chen said, suddenly short. "I will speak to the vice-minister. In the meantime, I suggest you do as I say. We all know what happened this morning. It's no longer safe for people to come here."

This gave my father pause. Maybe in trying to help he was only baiting the trap.

"Perhaps you're right."

The ambassador studied him. "So we're clear, then."

My father drew a breath. "Yes. Your Excellency."

———

Shortly after the ambassador left, the telephone rang.

"Feng-shan, it's Ruth."

My father started. Ruth and Max Blumberg were two of the many friends he had made since arriving in Vienna. As a diplomat, his circle was wide as a matter of course, immersed as he was in the life of the city, and he was an affable man versed in the art of conversation. He often held court in our sitting room, everyone staying up late until the room was miasmic with smoke (everyone, that is, except Grace, who always retired early). He last saw Ruth at a dance attended by Nazi officials. He couldn't tell if they knew the Blumbergs were Jewish—Germans seemed to condescend to Austrians in general—but when one of the otherwise solicitous officials took a leprous view of Viennese women, my father made a point of dancing with Ruth. It wasn't the first time they had danced. The previous winter they had been part of a group that had gone to Semmering, where they skied by day and danced by night. Ruth was a frank and witty woman who sympathized with Grace—"Must be hard to hear only gibberish"—in a way that meant she also felt for *him*. Months later, after dancing before Nazi officials, they stepped out for air and wound up leaning against a wall, she with one knee raised and her arms tucked behind her like wings. Something about her pose and the strangeness of the evening made him lean in for a kiss. Halfway to her, he stopped, drew back, from decency or fear, he could never decide. But she hadn't flinched, not in the slightest, which meant she wasn't opposed, or she simply hadn't realized. He was never sure which.

"Where are you?" he asked over the phone. "Are you all right?"

"I'm at home. I'm fine, we're fine. We've been spared so far, thank god. But it's terrible, what's happening."

The Blumbergs were among those who had held out, stayed on. They couldn't imagine living anywhere else, including the Dominican Republic, the one country that had opened its doors. And my father's descriptions of Shanghai—prostitutes, opium, gambling houses—had hardly made China seem enticing. But perhaps the time had come.

"Have you changed your minds?"

"Yes."

"Good."

"Can you come tonight?"

It took him a moment to realize what she was asking.

"We can't leave the house."

"No, of course not."

"Will you come, then?"

Decades later, on the balcony of the apartment on Russian Hill to which he had retired, my father admitted to weighing the risks. What if he were found out, relieved of his duties, sent back to China? What chance would he and Grace have then?

"Feng-shan, please. I'll do anything."

Perhaps it was just a turn of phrase corrupted by the memory of his own lust, but it sounded like a proposition, which startled and shamed him.

"How many should I bring?"

———

After my foray into the streets, I expected to be met at the door and berated, perhaps made to kneel on the floor of the entryway—a not uncommon punishment. Instead, I found Grace in her robe, one hand spread at the base of her throat, listening to Old Chao in the kitchen. Soon after, through the floor of my room, I heard her having a one-sided conversation, which I took to mean she had called my father. She asked how he was and how soon he'd be back and even offered to meet him, but by the sound of things he wouldn't let her.

I was trying to read comics in bed when the doorbell rang. Footsteps emerged from my parents' room and pattered down the stairs. Then a soft male voice I had never heard wafted up in English. When my father had guests, I was expected to greet them, but in this case something told me not to. Part of me wanted to see the American for myself, but another part of me was afraid, as if seeing him would betray once and for all what was happening.

For a while they talked in the sitting room. Then they came upstairs. I waited for a knock, expecting to be introduced, but all that came was the sound of a door shutting, then murmurs, then nothing. Ten, maybe fifteen minutes later they went back downstairs, where the front door closed with a snap.

When my father came home, I was there to greet him as usual. In my mind I had worked out ways to forewarn him, but when the time came I had no words. I simply watched as Old Chao delivered the news, only this time my father could no longer hide his feelings. "Grace, where are you?" he shouted. She appeared at the top of the stairs and clipped down in heels, fastening earrings as she went, as if she were merely running late.

"What was he doing here again?" my father asked.

"He wanted to say goodbye," Grace replied.

"Why didn't he do that yesterday?"

"Because he didn't know he was leaving. It was a different world yesterday."

For every question, she had a cool reply: He's an old friend. He speaks *English*. How can you begrudge me someone to *talk* to? All of these ready answers left my father flustered until he finally said, "You're being unfaithful."

Grace looked strangely satisfied. "You're one to talk."

My father's face slackened. At the time, I didn't know what this meant, only that Grace had parried and struck a blow. I kept waiting for him to reply, but he only looked at us plaintively. Then he opened the door and left.

———

At that hour the gas lamps were lit and the cobblestones long with shadows. A skim of cloud veiled the sky and trapped the moon in its own light. I don't know what my father was thinking or feeling as he walked away from our town house and through the Inner City. I can only imagine that he saw his own life mirrored in the wreckage around him, which steeled him to his real purpose in leaving.

The Blumbergs lived in the Second District. After crossing the inky waters of the Danube Canal, my father came to the Leopoldstadt district, also in shambles. On Leopoldstrasse he passed the remnants of a synagogue: Torah scrolls scattered like so much newsprint and the temple itself reduced to a blackened husk. He burrowed into his coat and pressed on.

After scanning left and right, he entered the Blumbergs' building, rapped on their door. He was greeted by silence, then shuffling, the stuttering scrape of a chair. A single scouring eye appeared at the door before the chain fell.

A young woman—the maid—opened the door and said, "*Grüss Gott.*"

Ruth crossed the room. "Feng-shan," she said, embracing him.

My father couldn't help noticing a coil of perfume. "Where's Max?"

"He's been taken away. For interrogation."

"My god."

"At least it was someone who works for him. You know Max, he's always good to his own. I think he'll be fine. He'll probably be back tonight." She smiled bravely.

"This will get him out," my father said, extracting papers from his coat.

She took them, examined them, then looked at my father, her eyes filming up. "Stay a while."

Max was an executive with the Standard Oil Company, and his home looked the part, especially the grand piano and the small tabletop radio—a novelty at the time. Ruth offered a cigarette and the maid brought coffee and schnapps and for a moment being there almost seemed pleasant. But after a bit of politesse—"How's Grace? And that sweet boy of yours?"—Ruth underscored the occasion by describing things she had seen and heard: friends beaten in the streets, a rabbi made to shout obscenities, a man forced to clean the sidewalk with his beard. "I have to applaud the Nazis," she said, "for the sheer inventiveness of their cruelty."

She rose and smoothed her brown housedress. "Come with me."

My father's pulse quickened when she led him to the bedroom. After closing the door, she crossed the room to a low-slung dresser and pulled out a jewelry box.

"I want Grace to have these," she said, plucking out jewelry as if pinching coins from a change purse.

"No," my father said, moving decisively toward her.

"I have more. We can't take everything."

My father put a hand on hers. After a long moment she dropped her things and gripped the edge of the dresser.

"It's not as if I have anyone to leave this to."

Toward the end of his life, after being widowed a second time, which had put him in a rare confessional mood, my father described being struck by the wild idea of gifting Ruth with a child, one she would carry with her all the way to Shanghai. Unlike that night at the dance, he no longer felt bound by his vows.

"Do you know what I want?" she asked, turning to him fiercely. "I want to come back and find everything as it was. I want to walk into my kitchen and take out my kettle and make myself a cup of tea. As if I never left."

She was hardly finished when they heard a knock on the door. The knock was urgent, as if someone being pursued were desperate to be let in. She and my father exchanged looks, then returned to the living room, where the maid was already approaching the door. Soon a brusque voice said, "What do you mean 'God greet you'? *Heil Hitler.*" Then two men in plainclothes barged in.

"Firearms search," one of them announced.

"We've already been searched," Ruth replied calmly. "Twice."

"Then we're searching again."

The man turned to my father. "Who are you?"

"A friend," he replied unhelpfully.

"What are you doing here?"

"Waiting for the man of the house."

The plainclothesman frowned. Among the reasons must have been my father's impeccable German. "Show your identification."

My father, seated again, released a veil of smoke. "By rights we should see yours first. Unless we're no longer following protocol."

The man's face contorted. "Our leader has said you foreigners no longer have special privileges. So you have no right to be so impudent."

The other man, gangling, pocked with acne scars, and impatient with the scene, began to stalk the apartment. Soon drawers were yanked, overturned, menageries of glass swept to the floor. Ruth tensed.

"You foreigners have taken what is rightfully ours," the first man continued, eyeing the room as if it were full of spoils. "What you saw last night was the outraged soul of the German people."

The man went on, grandiloquently.

Eventually the other returned, having failed, it seemed, to discover anything. "Who are you?" he said. Without waiting for the answer, he reached into his greatcoat, pulled out a revolver, and aimed it at my father.

My father had seen many things in his time—a man crippled by the Blue Mob in Shanghai, another executed by Communists on the streets of Changsha—but he had never looked down the barrel of a gun, and he stared with a mixture of curiosity and awe.

"Who are you?" the man repeated, voice rising.

The maid closed her eyes, mumbling.

"Who *are* you?"

This time my father detected a pleading: for the chance to put the gun down honorably.

"I'm the consul general of China."

The two men looked at each other in dismay. "Goddamn it. Why didn't you say so?"

With that, the men left as abruptly as they had come.

———

That night I ate dinner alone, wondering if Grace was right about my father. Once, in Changsha, I found a silver coin on my way home from school. When I got home I showed Grace, who promptly took it for "safekeeping." Feeling the money was rightfully mine, I took a dollar from my father's coat. When the money was discovered in my room, my father thrashed me with his belt, then fell to his knees begging me not to steal, which I found even more terrifying. All the while, I expected Grace to intercede, but she didn't.

So, despite his guilt-ridden look after Grace's accusation, I decided my father believed in character too much to be unfaithful and that the only one capable of deception was Grace.

After dinner I went upstairs, brushed my teeth, and changed into my nightclothes, all with a self-sufficiency that made me feel lonely. Then I shut off the lights and lay awake listening for the door. Eventually I was drawn to the window by shouts, tramping footsteps, the blare of klaxons, but all I could see through a scrawl of branches was Beethovenplatz in repose.

I was startled when the telephone rang. Grace came padding out of her room and down the stairs, but Old Chao, efficient as always, reached the phone first. From the top of the stairs I heard her asking who it was but didn't catch the answer.

Before long, the handle to the front door joggled in a ghostly way and my father appeared, surprised by the sight of Grace waiting there with her arms crossed. They greeted each other with the same look of injury and hauteur. Without removing his coat or hat, my father strode into the sitting room. From my perch on the stairs, unobserved, I saw him pour a drink.

"Ruth called."

My father looked up.

"Max is home. She said you would know what that meant. You went to see her, didn't you?"

My father sat down and took a vacant sip of his drink.

Slowly, haltingly, as if searching for ways not to, he recounted his day. It was at best a sketch whose details took decades to fill in, but that was the first time I heard about the ambassador and the visas, the Gestapo and the gun. At the first mention of Ruth, Grace scowled triumphantly, but by degrees she looked concerned, astonished, and finally chastened. When my father was done, he rubbed his eyes, and Grace sat down beside him. When at last she touched a hand to his shoulder, he turned and they looked at each other, and it seemed they had reached some kind of truce; whatever the reckoning, it wouldn't happen tonight. I was glad my father had been vindicated but pained to think that Grace might be forgiven, that our lives might simply go on as before.

————

Three months later we found ourselves at Vienna West Station, under plumes of smoke and ash and a canopy of iron and glass. In the weeks and months after those two nights of chaos, my father had continued to sign visas until he was found out and a black mark placed in his file. That's when he decided to go back to China. Grace, however, wasn't going with us. She was going back to America, and we were there to see her off. The three of us formed an awkward circle on the platform, next to an arcade where soldiers with dogs stood sentry. We didn't hug or kiss, much less cry. We simply waited for the moment of release, for the frayed tether to finally snap.

As we stood there, a line of children shuffled past, large

manila labels dangling from their necks. Each carried a suitcase save for the ones so young they needed to be carried themselves. Their parents watched resolutely from the other side of the arcade, unwilling to give the soldiers who kept them off the platform the pleasure of a scene. Grace turned, tracked the children, then looked at my father. To be parting now, as others were being parted, was the final measure of their failure. As if cleaved by the thought, she hurried onto the train.

Clouds of soot issued from the smokebox, and with a slow-waking lurch the train began to move. As it left the station, I thought of the time after my mother's death when my father left me to go to Chicago. He was gone a long time, nearly six months, and each day I would go to the window, wondering when he was coming back. Now those children, too, would have to wait. That day, the war not yet begun, I believed what their parents had said outside the platform: *Be good. We'll see you soon.*

The train slowly dwindled, and I thought we would go. I was ready to go anywhere, do anything, now that I had my father back. But he stood where he was, watching the train reach its vanishing point, his hat pushed up in a tousled way. Only then did I stop to wonder what he must have been feeling, coming to the end of something that had had its beginnings, however inexplicably, in joy. Even when the train became little more than a wisp of smoke, he kept staring. I see him still, gazing into the distance, mourning all that couldn't be saved.

Everything In Between

W HEN I WAS YOUNG, THE CHINESE OF PORT ELIZABETH
were granted use of a beach near the village of Schoen-
makerskop. In some ways it was a mean little beach, jagged
and scrubby and nothing at all like the golden sands of Algoa
Bay on the other side of the cape, but we loved the Schoenies
and went there often, especially around Christmas and New
Year's Day, at the height of summer, our arms laden with gear,
with baskets and lawn chairs and tackle, our fathers in belted
trunks with matching shirts, our mothers in headscarves and
daring high-waisted bikinis. At low tide, the rocky shore was
safe enough for toddling, and I still remember myself in a
nubby pink suit, poking through rock pools and splashing in
gullies as dolphins leaped in the bay. Even now, when I yearn
for the sea, I visit that beach, if only in memory.

Next to our beach was a fishing pier, a long, thin wooden

jetty that stretched out on pilings. Unlike other fathers, Ah Ba taught his daughter how to fish. I learned how to hold the rod and work the reel and, in time, to cast with a rod of my own. From a young age, I knew I had to stay in our section of the pier, behind the sign that forbade us from going beyond, even though I longed to cast in deep water, where the fishing was best. Perhaps because of me, Ah Ba always stationed himself closer to shore, where he often laughed with the men who were not allowed in turn to enter our section and practically had to fish over the rocks. Still, we managed to catch blacktail and shad and sometimes enormous kob. My favorite, though, was bronze bream: tawny and flat and small enough to bring in myself.

The summer I was eight, my family made a trip to the Schoenies in our two-toned Holden Special, aqua blue with a white roof and white stripes along each side. As we sped down a single lane through open grassland, the wind in my hair, my brother in my lap, Ah Ma turned to Ah Ba and said, "I think it's time we bought a house."

Ah Ba was a quiet man, slow to speech. He kept his eyes on the road and didn't reply for so long that I thought he hadn't heard.

"Where?" he finally asked.

"Some other part of town."

We lived in Kabega, the Chinese area of Port Elizabeth, a subdivision surrounded by farmland. It hadn't occurred to me that Ah Ma wanted a house somewhere other than our neighborhood.

"How?" Ah Ba asked.

"They're issuing permits now. As long as the neighbors agree."

"Why would we put ourselves—"

"For *them*," Ah Ma said, dipping her head at the back seat.

"They're happy at school."

"What good is Chinese school? They need to learn in English. Or Afrikaans."

Ah Ba drove on in silence, and I thought the matter had dropped. Then he said, "We're not White."

Ah Ma looked away, hair whipping. "That's what you always say."

Her voice was bitter, and I didn't understand why she seemed to resent something that seemed self-evident. But I felt her exerting pressure, as she had a way of doing, and somehow I knew that Ah Ba would relent.

———

When Ah Ba was eighteen, he was accepted to medical school in Hong Kong, but when the Japanese invaded, he could no longer attend. So he applied to the only two medical schools in the country, Witwatersrand and Cape Town, and to his surprise he got into both. Because his family had roots near Johannesburg, he chose Wits.

At the start of term, Ah Ba rode up Hospital Hill on a trolley bus, suitcase in hand. From the upper deck, he caught his first glimpse of the medical school, a three-story granite building with inlaid brick on the ground floor. After stepping inside, he was greeted by a pale young man wearing round tortoiseshell glasses who found Ah Ba's name on a list and flushed. You see, when my great-grandfather came to labor for gold in the mines of Randfontein, a clerk in Durban, his port of entry, had translated his given name, Cheuk-man, as Chapman, and we've been Chapmans ever since.

The residence hall was equally surprised, but everyone there was polite. Ah Ba was offered a chair and a glass of water as others conferred. Then he was told he could stay until he found other housing. Ah Ba rose from his seat, picked up his suitcase, and said, "No, thank you."

He spent the next six years in school while living in Ferreirastown, in a room above a Chinese butcher that smelled like an abattoir. Upon closer inspection, the medical school was rather derelict, overrun by high grass and weedy patches of marigolds. Despite grand ambitions, the architect had neglected to provide for water, air, and gas for laboratories, so they had to be housed elsewhere. Worse, there were certain patients Ah Ba wasn't allowed to treat, certain cadavers he wasn't allowed to touch. While others did rounds at the Fever Hospital, Queen Victoria Maternity, and Johannesburg General, he and two others were consigned to the Non-European Hospital. Though suspicion was not uncommon among Blacks, Indians, and Chinese, the three of them became great mates, Ah Ba and those I would come to call Uncle Menzi and Uncle Dalvir.

For much of their time in school, the world was at war. Many of their classmates joined the South African Medical Corps, and the three of them felt compelled to do the same. During the school year, they trained on weekends; over July winter break, they trundled out on lorries to Zonderwater and tended to Italian POWs, captured on the North and East African fronts. Their first year, Zonderwater had been a tent city; in time it became a full-scale detention camp with schools, theaters, tennis courts, football fields, and the largest military hospital in the Union. Some refused to let Ah Ba and his mates administer smallpox and typhoid shots, but for the most part the prisoners, well fed in their white shirts, khakis, and side caps, were friendly, pliant, and desperate for home. Those who died were buried in a field of white crosses.

During the war, the old warhorse, Jan Smuts, was reelected—Allied fortunes had improved, and the country wanted a steady hand—but in 1948, when he stood yet again, the country's mood had shifted: the economy was weak, and Afrikaners feared both British immigration and *Swart gevaar*—Black peril—and he was accused of quietly supporting integration. There was only one alternative to what the Nationalists called "suicide."

"What is this 'apartness' of which they speak?" Uncle Menzi asked during the first of their many reunions.

"I've had quite enough apartness already, thank you very much," said Uncle Dalvir, to laughter.

Ah Ba and Uncle Menzi couldn't vote, but they weren't

especially worried about the outcome. Yes, the National and Afrikaner parties were expected to gain seats, but not enough to tip the balance of power. The day after the election, the papers were still unaware of what had happened. It took another day to realize that despite winning fewer than half the votes, D. F. Malan was prime minister.

In 1948, Ah Ma was only thirteen. She had spent her life in the family shop in South End near the center of Port Elizabeth. The shop was a whitewashed building with a colonnade and wrought-iron bars over the windows. Besides the usual—mealie meal, sweets, cooldrinks—her family grew and sold their own Chinese vegetables. Many poor Whites also patronized the shop, if somewhat sheepishly. Not long after the election, one such woman came in, hair done, back straight.

"Order," she said, looking at Ah Ma. "From now on there will be order."

My parents didn't meet for another twelve years. One day Ah Ba happened upon the shop and found Ah Ma standing with her arms crossed and her pretty lips pursed as someone tried to haggle, and apparently that was that. Within a year they were married.

I wonder, though, if that was the whole story. When I was five or six, I found a photo of a woman whose hair was so light it looked colorless. When I asked Ah Ba who she was, he studied the photo intently before putting it back in the drawer. The medical school had had a small common room for women, and I've often wondered if that's where they met, if they had been something other than friends, and if one of the first rules of apartness, the law against mixed marriages, had brought them to an end.

For a few years, my parents were able to live in the city center, but in 1966, when I was three and Ah Ma pregnant with my brother, they were finally forced to move. Twenty years earlier, some entrepreneurial Chinese had built a school on Cape Road, about eight miles west of the city center, and this became the basis for settling all Chinese in Kabega. My own memories of Kabega are pleasant. I liked walking to school and living close to my friends. It seemed like everything I would ever need existed within a few square miles. I especially remember the woman who raised chickens in her yard. Whenever we went, my brother and I were allowed to run around the yard till we caught one. The woman would then take the chicken inside, bring its squawking to an end, and hand it back to us in a still-warm sack, which brushed our legs on the way home.

Maybe Ah Ma would have accepted Kabega if she'd still had the shop, but after her part of South End was cleared, it was razed. The sign that had read FAMILY GROCERS / GENERAL DEALERS for over sixty years came down with one paw of the excavator. She'd given her life to that shop, hadn't finished school because of it. Now all she had was a two-bedroom flat that no one had ever asked for.

———

When we got to the beach, Ah Ma took me into one of the change rooms built by the Chinese, complete with Chinese signs. As I stood on cool concrete, she helped me into my suit. This one was yellow and orange. I'd long outgrown my pink one.

"You're getting so big, Julia," she said. "Time for your own room, don't you think?"

I knew what she was doing and said nothing.

At that moment, one of Ah Ma's friends, Auntie Sung, burst into the room in a wide-brimmed hat and sunglasses, and I ran off to play with my brother. The tide was out, and we clambered over rocks covered with rusty lichen. By the time we wandered back for something from the cooler box, Ah Ma and Auntie Sung were sunning in webbed lawn chairs and deep in conversation.

"Why don't you just leave like everyone else?" Auntie Sung asked. "That's what I would do."

"Where would you go?"

"Canada. I have a cousin in Toronto."

"Isn't it cold there?"

Auntie Sung shrugged. "Australia, then. America."

"We've lived here so long," Ah Ma said. "And we can't go *back*."

It wasn't just that none of us had ever set foot in China; everyone knew that strange convulsions in that distant country made going back impossible.

"I know it's bad there," Auntie Sung said, "but I don't understand why they keep smuggling themselves *here*. I want to say, 'Stop! Go anywhere else!'"

"Things are changing. We can live in different areas now."

"What? You think you're better than Blacks?"

"Blacks?" Ah Ma said. "We're better than Whites."

Auntie Sung tossed her head back and cackled. I had heard Ah Ma say things like "Black ghosts" and "White devils," but never in public, and I felt a current go through me.

I walked out to the pier and found Ah Ba standing at an easy distance from the other men, a couple of silvery shad silently heaving in a bucket.

"I don't want to move," I said.

Ah Ba looked at me, hair matted in the breeze. I expected him to say, *I don't want to move, either*, but all he did was hand me the rod.

———

Two weeks later, there was a knock at our door. When Ah Ma answered, a woman in a flared green pantsuit appeared in the doorway, her dark hair feathered.

"You must be Mrs. Chapman," she said, extending a hand. "I'm Valerie."

Earlier that morning, Ah Ma had dropped off my brother at Auntie Sung's. As soon as she got back, she put me into a dress and Ah Ba into a suit.

"Let's see what we have here," Valerie said, eyeing our kitchen and living room. We lived in a complex of two-story buildings built by the Department of Community Development. "Better than a paraffin stove," she said. "But we can do better still."

We followed her out to her station sedan and got in the back seat. "We'll start in Linton Grange and Bramhope," she said as she drove. "Those are your neighbors. They already know and trust you."

Ah Ma and Ah Ba exchanged looks. When Kabega was first proposed as the Chinese group area, nearby residents had objected.

In Linton Grange, the streets had pretty names: Lavender, Petunia, Hydrangea. As we drove past low-slung stucco houses, faces looked up from mailboxes, garden hoses. Under the pass laws, we didn't have to carry the *dompas*—the dumb pass, as the Bantu called it—but somehow I knew that Valerie was our passbook.

Eventually we reached a wide, double-gabled house with a FOR SALE sign outside. Valerie opened the gate to the yard while the three of us hung back, instinctively. As Ah Ba shifted, Ah Ma draped an arm over my shoulder and flattened a hand against my chest. The gesture was unfamiliar, and I couldn't tell if she was striking a pose, protecting me, or both.

The front door opened and an elderly man in thick black glasses emerged. As soon as he saw us, his face screwed. *"Maak jy 'n grap?"* he asked. A stormy exchange ensued. The only thing I managed to catch was Valerie saying, *"Hulle is die Chapmans."*

When the door shut, she rapped again, to no avail. She came back down the walk, stepped past us, and slipped into the car, and we followed suit.

She sat in the driver's seat, breathing hard. Then she started the car and said, "Maybe that wasn't the best idea."

———

The following weekend, we set off again in Valerie's car, only this time for Bramhope Road, where we came to a simple white house with a Spanish roof that sat across from a field. "The fewer neighbors, the better," Valerie said, eyeing the bush. She'd assured us on the drive over that no one would be surprised. Apparently the owners were "motivated."

A harried-looking woman answered the door with a towheaded baby stuck to her hip. She unlocked the grille and flicked a smile as I passed, which made me like her. We stepped through the foyer and into the living room, where two older children, a boy and a girl, were playing, the floor around them strewn with dolls and so many die-cast Dinky Toys that my brother would have gone mad.

Though they hardly deigned to look up, Ah Ma fawned over the children and said, "We have a son, too. We didn't bring him . . ."

But we could have, I thought.

Valerie led us into the kitchen, where the fridge and

stove were nearly the same aqua blue as our car. Then she led us down the hall to the bedrooms. When I saw that the girl had a room of her own, with a headboard full of books, I stirred with desire. Maybe Ah Ma was right.

When we circled back to the living room, Ah Ma drew a breath. The woman was sitting on her couch, blouse open, her baby hoisted to the swell of her breast. Ah Ba looked away, but I was so enthralled that Ah Ma said *"Mo tai"* and turned my head like a lid on a jar.

"Well?" the woman asked.

Valerie said, "We'll need to—"

"We like it," said Ah Ma.

"Then I need twenty thousand rand."

Valerie raised a brow. "You have an offer?"

The woman didn't reply.

"It's listed for nineteen."

"I need twenty."

"Let's go," Ah Ba said, starting for the door.

"Yes, let's," Valerie said.

"I thought you said he was a doctor," the woman said, squinting.

"He is," Valerie replied.

"That's fine," Ah Ma said. "Twenty is fine."

We showed ourselves out. When we reached the car, Valerie said, "Why don't we give your parents a moment?" and led me into the field. As we walked toward the scraggly reach of some buffalo thorn, a car door shut and muffled voices rose from within.

"Do you like the house?" Valerie asked.

"Yes," I said, thinking of the headboard.

She smiled. "Then maybe it's worth twenty."

We went back to the car, where all three adults conferred. Then, for some reason, we all started for the house next door. I thought I saw curtains ruffling, but when we knocked, no one answered.

Valerie chewed a corner of her lip. "Let's try the other neighbors, then."

We approached the house on the other side, where a woman with a regal perm appeared in a housedress. When Valerie explained why we were there, the woman waved us in, hurriedly, as if we were being spied on.

"Of course I'll sign, my dear," she said, clutching Ah Ma by the shoulders. "It's preposterous that you should have to ask."

Ah Ma, who had stiffened at the touch, said, "My husband's a doctor."

"I don't doubt it," the woman said. "But it doesn't matter. It doesn't matter at all. What did the other neighbors say?"

"They're not home."

"Leave the papers with me. I'll make sure they sign."

We went home and waited for word. With each passing day, Ah Ma leaped more anxiously for the phone while Ah Ba's mood seemed to lighten. In the end, though, Valerie called to say that the other neighbors had finally agreed, and suddenly Ah Ma rallied while Ah Ba grew morose. Quietly, I dreamed of the headboard, which I thought was now mine.

Two days later, the phone rang. "Hi, Valerie," Ah Ma said. And then her face darkened. "What do you mean?" she said, and a pall fell over the room. Even Ah Ba looked concerned as he turned down the radio.

"But we were there first," Ah Ma said weakly.

Valerie's voice chittered through the flat. I couldn't make out a word of it, but I knew the permit had taken too long.

————

We had no appointments the following weekend. That's because Uncle Menzi and Uncle Dalvir were coming to visit. Over the years, Ah Ba and his mates had gotten together whenever they could, a tradition that continued, if less frequently, now that Uncle Dalvir lived in East Pakistan.

Ah Ba went to the airport and returned with Uncle Dalvir, who looked natty in a bell-bottomed suit, his mustache as neat as ever, but his eyes were dark from the long journey, made longer by having to fly through Tel Aviv and around airspace where South African Airways was banned. Nonetheless, he greeted us in his wry way: "I don't believe we've met, good sir," he said, extending a hand to my brother, whom he hadn't seen in three years. "Jonathan! No, it can't be!"

When Uncle Menzi arrived from Durban, he gave all of us a fierce embrace. Ah Ma stiffened, much as she had the weekend before, maybe because Uncle Menzi had grown heavier over the years, to the point where he seemed to enfold her.

At dinnertime, the adults sat in the dining room while my brother and I ate in the living room. Earlier that day, we had gone to see the woman with the chickens, and Ah Ma had spent the afternoon in the kitchen. As I kneeled at the coffee table, sipping on a chocolatey glass of Milo, which Ah Ma reserved for special occasions, Uncle Dalvir expanded on life in Dacca. I was especially keen to know how his spirited daughters, Fariha and Shompa, whom I used to play with, were doing in school. When he described the recent cyclone that had drowned half a million in the Ganges Delta, he dropped his voice so that I couldn't hear.

At some point, Uncle Menzi was asked, "How are things at the university?"

After medical school at Wits and a mandatory one-year hospital internship, Uncle Menzi had gone into general practice in East London, on the coast between Port Elizabeth and Durban. For all of them, general practice had been preferable to working in a hospital, where they would have been paid less and couldn't have risen to instructing nurses and junior medics. Two years ago, however, Uncle Menzi had accepted a teaching post at the University of Natal, where a segregated Black medical faculty had been established in the fifties.

He shook his head despondently. "The students, they struggle, truly."

Unlike Uncle Menzi, who had gone to boarding school in Lesotho, most of his students came from schools in the Bantustans. "We added a preliminary year to help them, but many still cannot make it past year two. They find anatomy and physiology difficult, especially when English and Afrikaans are their second and third languages."

Ah Ma's ears perked up. "So language is important."

"Very important," Uncle Menzi said, unaware of Ah Ba's sidelong glance at Ah Ma. "Fewer than half our students go on to graduate."

"A good school makes a difference," Ah Ma said.

"All the difference," Uncle Menzi said.

———

That night, my brother and I slept on the couch while our uncles slept in our room—uncomfortably, I could only imagine, on our skinny beds, each of them troubling the other with their night sounds. They were up early, though, and out the door before I awoke. Ah Ba had chartered a boat, and I pictured the three of them casting off the cape, at the farthest point of the breakwater, governed by nothing but sea and sky.

They returned that evening in high spirits: all of them had caught garrick. Later I would see a photo of the three of them on shore, each cradling a shimmering trophy at least three feet long. It wasn't just success but the symmetry of their success that made them smile in triplicate.

They were gone most of the next day, too, out again on the water, but I still felt their presence, and the way their presence transformed the mood, and the evening was again filled with food and drink and stories of the past, many of which I had heard before and would hear again, tales of war and hardship and youth, stories that made them laugh but also grieve time's passing. So much had changed, and so little, too.

In the morning, Uncle Menzi drove back to Durban while Uncle Dalvir went to see relatives in Johannesburg, and the flat descended into gloom.

"If we had a house, we'd have more room for guests," Ah Ma said.

After considering, Ah Ba said, "Why live where friends need permits to visit?"

———

Valerie had a new plan: find a house in Richmond Hill, one of the oldest neighborhoods in the city. Proximity had not helped our cause, so why not venture farther afield?

Before our first viewing, Ah Ma put me into a starchy blue dress with a Peter Pan collar, then clamped my face, her eyes trembling.

"Be good," she said. "I need you to be good."

We drove to the city center. When the soaring red brick of the Campanile came into view, we turned off Cape Road and onto a street of gingerbread houses, and to my amazement we stopped in front of one, part of a row, seven or eight by my count, all with inset balconies and pretty scrollwork. An agent was there to meet us, a man with wispy hair who shook our hands and showed us in.

The town house was narrow, with plank floors, bead-board ceilings, and a cast-iron fireplace. Upstairs, the ceilings sloped, but the balcony let in light and offered a glimpse of the bay—something even Ah Ba seemed to appreciate.

This time, Valerie had thought to make appointments with the neighbors, so we went directly next door. An older couple greeted us, their smiles pinched, the husband ruddy-faced, the wife dowdy and shapeless in a polyester housecoat. We were invited in, less out of kindness, it seemed, than want of something to say.

We were served tea in the living room, in a version of the house we had just seen, the couple ensconced on the couch, the rest of us on chairs, including two dragged in from the dining room. The couple was dismally quiet, so Valerie conducted the interview herself, and Ah Ba obliged by naming his profession, alma mater, and service during the war. With each new revelation, the man turned to his wife uncertainly, wondering on what grounds they could possibly say no.

As the adults talked, I sipped my tea. The only tea I'd ever had was bitter, but this tea was creamy and sweet and came in a delicate rose-patterned cup. From her armchair, Ah Ma gave me a warning look, but I didn't know why. My little feet swung in their Mary Janes.

When I set my empty cup on the coffee table, the wife rose from the couch and reached for the teapot.

"Julia," Ah Ma said, looking at me, "I think that's enough."

But the woman fixed me another cup as if she hadn't heard, and I found myself in a bind. I couldn't well drink the tea against Ah Ma's wishes, but I couldn't ignore it, either, so I took a few cautious sips and resolved to leave the rest—to be good. As I lowered my cup to the table, I kept my eyes on its swirling contents, but something about the effort, the overconcentration, made me lose focus. When I set the cup down, the table wasn't where I expected it to be, and the cup slipped from my hand.

"Julia!" Ah Ma cried, leaping to her feet.

I heard a damp patter. Then all was commotion.

———

For the rest of the day, I lay in bed while my parents' voices thumped through the walls. Sometimes their voices were muddled, other times piercingly clear:

"Rise, yes, but rise together."

"What good are your principles if they harm your children?"

"They need to know right from wrong."

"Well, I can't live like this anymore."

They carried on for days, and I thought I had broken something between them, a feeling that only deepened when Ah Ba asked me to go for a drive, the two of us alone, something we never did. As we traced our familiar route to the Schoenies—a drive I can still make in my sleep—I was sure that Ah Ba was leaving us, and I tried not to cry.

It was now late summer and a weeknight besides, so we had the pier to ourselves. Nonetheless, we stayed in our section. For a long time we stood there taking in the sea, its sheer immensity, the railing still warm from the day's heat.

At last Ah Ba said, "We're moving."

My whole body unclenched. "Where?"

"Australia."

I blinked and blinked, then looked back out to sea. When I was younger, I used to imagine that I could see all the way to Antarctica. We lived on the edge of the world, but when you're a child, wherever you are is the center of everything.

"Why?" I asked, meaning why Australia and not Canada, England, America?

"Because I want your mother to be happy."

We listened to the waves, their endless crashing. When my eyes filmed, Ah Ba said, "It's not your fault."

This only made my chin quiver, even though I knew—and still believe—that it wasn't just my blunder that had cost us.

———

On the day of our departure, Auntie Sung came to say goodbye.

"You're doing the right thing," she said. "It's time to go."

Within a year she, too, would leave—for Toronto. In Johannesburg, we got on a plane bound for Mauritius. There was a time when the Wallaby service only went on to Perth, but now it went all the way to Sydney, so that's where we made our home. We bought a house in Surry Hills, not far, ironically, from Haymarket and the Chinese shops on Dixon Street. In time, Ah Ba rebuilt his practice, treating far less malnutrition and far more heart disease, and didn't retire until he was in his seventies. Ah Ma, for her part, took courses through Technical and Further Education and eventually opened a shop in Ashfield, where I still like to go for fresh fish on weekends, though the shop is no longer ours. My brother and I both went to uni, and I went on to teach at a state school. We're both married, and our children all eat Chiko Rolls and watch footy. I am, of course, leaving out a good deal. It wasn't always easy, but we made the best of things. And when we saw the final and still more terrible paroxysms of apartness on television, we felt we had in fact done the right thing. But these days when I visit Ah Ma in the nursing home, she stares off into the distance, eyes viscid, and I know what she's thinking about. The veld. The sea. Ah Ba.

I was born on one continent; I will die on another. This is the story of many. It's everything in between that's different. Who would I have become if we had landed in Perth? If my parents had chosen Toronto, London, San Francisco? And what if friction and gravity had been kinder the year I was eight? What country, then, might yet have been ours?

Belsize Park

Y OU SHOULD COME TO LONDON AT THE END OF TERM. MEET
my parents."

We were lying in bed in her room overlooking the High
Street. A month earlier, we had gone down to London to see
a band at the Half Moon in Putney, but we hadn't made our
presence known to her parents, who lived in Belsize Park.
I had agreed: no need for introductions yet. But apparently
the time had come.

"Really?"

"Why not? We're going on six months."

This wasn't exactly true. We had met at the end of second year and rendezvoused intently for a few weeks before
going our separate ways for the summer, I to Stoke-on-Trent
to work in my parents' takeaway—Lucky House, it was
called—and she to France to summer with her family, with

no particular understanding between us. Come autumn, we did start up again right away, but all told, we'd only been together for a term.

"My parents need my help in the shop."

A little moue appeared on her face. "Can't they spare you for a day or two?"

In the beginning, I couldn't quite believe I had fallen in with someone like Fiona, so clever and lovely and thoroughly English. The only way to manage my fear of losing her was to take that loss as a given. Since London, though, we'd spent nearly every day together, and despite myself I'd started to hope for more. If I hesitated, it was only to be sure she wasn't just being polite. But her little pout told me all I needed to know.

"All right, I'll go. But only if you come to Stoke."

She stilled, recalibrating. "Will your parents like me?"

I wasn't sure, but I said, "They'll love you."

———

My first week at Oxford, I had sat high in the upper gallery at the Sheldonian in full academic dress, listening to the vice-chancellor intone gravely in Latin and feeling as I often had in grammar school, that I was an interloper and none of this was my birthright. That same week, I wandered the deluged stalls at Freshers' Fair but couldn't bring myself to join the Pooh Sticks Club or the Heterosexual Decadence Society or even the Chinese Students Association, despite the doe-eyed looks of the two young women behind the table. Instead, I spent most of first year alone in my room or in a study carrel at the Bodleian Library where, amid all those rare and ancient books, I had to swear an oath not to "kindle flame."

In second year, though, I found myself a coterie of friends who took an equally cynical view of the goings-on around us, the college balls especially, but at the end of Trinity term, we decided, for a lark, to crash one. The men went down to Shepherd and Woodward on the High to rent evening wear, in the spirit of Achaeans entering a Trojan Horse. But when I put on the black tie and tailcoat and looked in the mirror, there in the privacy of the dressing room, I thought for the first time, *I could be one of them.*

When the time came, we infiltrated the milling crowd at Radcliffe Square, with its battlements and spires, burnished at that hour in deep shades of gold. A row of women in taffeta posed for pictures in front of the Radcliffe Camera. One had thin, straight, mousy hair, this at a time when hair was all about volume, and her décolletage sagged, which made my heart go out to her. I caught her eye and saw myself refracted: tall, reedy, exotic. Then the moment passed and we both looked away.

Later, after I had breached security and found myself in a lantern-lit quad, I saw her again, this time standing alone, peering over the rim of her glass and looking rather abandoned. "Hello again," she said, which should have bolstered my confidence. Instead, I mumbled the usual: Hello, how are you, which college are you at? When she told me, I cooled. If any college still embodied the spirit of bright young things, it was Magdalen.

"What about you?"

"Lady Margaret Hall."

"The women's college?"

I bristled. I was proud of LMH and the fact that it was on the outskirts of town—orbital, like me.

"We have something now called co-education," I said.

My comment struck the mark, a little too well, it seemed. She took an injured sip of her drink, and I waited for her to flag down a friend and flee. Instead, she described her years in boarding school as part of a flotsam of girls in an endless sea of boys. Her school didn't have a girls' house; rather, every house had a couple of girls in each A-level year, and they had been tormented. "It's no better here," she said bitterly. "My junior common room debated the motion 'College women should be hired out on the same basis as punts.' It's astonishing."

My ears burned, and the only thing I could think to do was tell her about grammar school, how my only friend was a boy named Ramesh and how we had gotten all the usual abuse. I thought it might have been too little, too late, but she softened, said, "That's awful," and something like recognition passed between us.

We kept talking. In time, standing gave way to sitting, and sitting in turn to lying down once we had vowed to make it all the way to the champagne breakfast. There would soon be far greater intimacies between us, yet in some ways nothing surpassed that first intimacy, the two of us lying face to face, right there in the quad, in full view of the dwindling ball, Fiona feeling safe enough to close her eyes and fall asleep.

———

From the time I was old enough to peer over the counter, I'd spent long hours at the front of my parents' takeaway. The summer Fiona and I were apart was no different. But unlike the summer before or the many years before that, when I whiled away the hours dreaming vaguely but intently of love, all my restive longing that summer took the form of someone real. When the school year ended, I said I would write, but she didn't know where her family would be staying in Paris and couldn't remember the address of their summer house in Colmar, so all I could do was give her mine. Every time the shop door chimed, I looked up hoping to see her, and every day I waited for the post, hoping for the smallest word.

At the end of each night, after my parents and I had trudged upstairs to our flat above the takeaway, I would retreat to my room and listen to records on my old Garrard Zero, and the track I played the most was "The Paris Match" by the Style Council. The song was a moody ballad about wandering the streets of Paris, looking for a lost lover, the match that had lit the fire. I liked the version sung by a woman, sad-eyed Tracey Thorn, which made it easier to imagine that Fiona was out there looking for me.

At the end of the summer, I finally received a postcard of brightly colored houses lining a canal. Fiona wrote breezily of dry heat and mountains and drinking Alsatian wine, her words circumnavigating the card in ever finer script. She said nothing about us, but I didn't care. She hadn't forgotten me.

———

As soon as Michaelmas term ended, Fiona and I took the train to Paddington Station. We'd done the same on our first trip to London six weeks before, sat rocking side by side on rough-hewn upholstery as the chalk and scattered scrub of the Chilterns streamed past, but the feeling then was different. Then, we'd had London—the whole wide world—to ourselves. This time, I was hurtling toward a brambly sense of entanglement, and the feeling sat uneasily.

Fiona's father came to retrieve us in his Vauxhall Cavalier, a hearteningly ordinary car for a banker. He pressed his graying beard to his daughter's cheeks, and his evident joy in seeing her extended itself to me. Belsize Park was a suburb near the heath, blanched by row upon row of white villas. Theirs was semidetached with a pebbled front garden and a raised ground floor.

"Mum, we're home!" Fiona cried as we stepped through the door.

From somewhere below came audible instructions to

the cook, instructions that seemed prolonged, as if we were being made to wait. Then footsteps rose from the lower ground floor, and her mother appeared in a navy-blue dress and pearls, her hair short and peppery. She accepted Fiona's kisses with hands hooked, like a mantis.

"You must be Peter," she said, flicking a smile, eyes darting.

"Pleasure to meet you, Mrs. Turner."

By way of welcome, she showed me the reception rooms. Both had a fireplace and a chandelier and dark, scrolled furnishings. Then she led me up not one but two flights of stairs to the uppermost floor, where I was shown to my room, floral as a garden. Fiona made as if to speak, then thought better of it.

Her mother said, "I hope this will do."

"Yes, of course. It's lovely. Thank you very much."

When we were alone, Fiona pressed her forehead to my shoulder. "I'm sorry."

"No, it's fine," I said, thinking how in Stoke we would have to share a room, since there would be nowhere else to put her.

———

The dining room was downstairs, on the lower ground floor, an open space with two sliding glass doors and a large picture window, all of which looked out onto the garden. On my way in, I passed the cook finishing off in the kitchen, a woman of indeterminate middle age who greeted me warmly. The dining room table was long; I sat across from Fiona while her parents sat at either end. After raising our glasses, we started on the Sunday roast, and I wasn't sure whether to speak or only speak when spoken to.

"This is lovely," I finally ventured. "And you have a lovely home."

"Do you know where the name 'Belsize' comes from?" Mr. Turner asked. "From the phrase *bel assis*. French for 'beautifully situated.'"

"It is," I said.

"This neighborhood is nearly a thousand years old. Ethelred the Unready granted the manor of Hampstead in 986—"

"Dad."

"—part of which later became the manor of Belsize. Richard Steele had a cottage on Haverstock Hill. Queen Victoria came out here for country drives."

I was compelled to say, "I grew up on Gerrard Street in the building where John Dryden once lived," then heard how strange that sounded. But Mr. Turner just smiled.

"And how did you come to live on Gerrard Street?"

"Here we go," Fiona said.

I flashed her a look to say it was fine. "My father moved to Chinatown when he came to London in the early sixties." Dad had been a rice farmer in the New Territories, I explained, squeezed out by the so-called vegetable revolution, and the only work he could find was in catering.

"I thought your parents lived in Stoke."

"They do now. My mother worked in catering, too, but they didn't like working for others, so they scrimped and saved and started their own takeaway. But it wasn't easy. They weren't just competing against other Chinese but Indians, Italians, and Cypriots. Plus Sainsbury's, Tesco, and M and S, which started making Chinese ready meals—"

"You have something in common with Mum," Fiona said happily. "She doesn't like Tesco, either."

Mrs. Turner cleared her throat and stiffened, now that the spotlight was on her. "I'm part of a preservation society here in Belsize Park."

"And they don't want Tesco moving in," Fiona said. "It wouldn't be . . . consistent with the character of the neighborhood."

"It wouldn't be," her father said. "Next thing you know, the streets will be full of lorries and car parks and we'll go the way of American cities."

Fiona smiled, as if she had goaded them. "Sorry, Peter. I interrupted you."

"Where was I? Yes, too much competition, so my parents moved farther and farther from Gerrard Street. When I was nine, we moved to Birmingham, but even Brum was too crowded, so we moved to Stoke. If you've ever wondered why Chinese run takeaways in every lonely corner of the world . . ."

"So your parents met in London," Mrs. Turner said, taking a different interest.

"Actually, no. After a year, Dad went back to Hong Kong

and married Mum. But the funny thing is, they could have met here."

"How's that?"

"My grandfather—Mum's dad—worked as a stoker on the Blue Funnel Line, which sailed between Hong Kong and Liverpool. During the war, he was part of the Merchant Navy. Helped to win the Battle of the Atlantic. He would have liked to stay after the war, but he was . . . repatriated."

"Killed?"

"No, deported."

After a silence, Mrs. Turner glanced at her husband and said, "Both our fathers served in the war."

"Yes, of course," I said.

———

At the end of the evening, I let Fiona and her mother catch up. After the pudding, Mr. Turner had excused himself and retired to his study, at which point the evening had entered a different phase, Mrs. Turner more relaxed somehow, maybe because the meal had come off.

Nonetheless, I lay in bed replaying the day, wondering how I'd done, if I'd said too much or too little. Eventually a knock came, and Fiona peered through the door. When she stepped in, I laughed. In Oxford, she lounged around in knickers and large off-the-shoulder T-shirts; here she wore a flannel nightgown, as floral as my bedspread.

"Look, it's Laura Ashley."

She smiled ruefully, slipping into bed.

"How'd I do?"

"You were brilliant, darling."

"Was I?"

"Yes. Sometimes my parents need to . . . *see* themselves, you know?"

"I just hope they like me."

"They do, they do," she said, pressing her lips to mine, softly at first, then more ardently, with no intention of stopping.

"What about your parents?" I whispered.

At this, she sat astride me, crossed her arms, and pulled off her nightgown, tousling her hair in the process.

"Never mind my parents," she said.

———

By the time we awoke, we had the house to ourselves, her father off to work and her mother off to a meeting—the preservation society, perhaps. Today was our only full day before we would leave for Stoke.

"Let's go shopping," she said over breakfast.

"Didn't you want to show me the heath?"

"I do. But let's go shopping first. I need to get gifts for my parents."

We got off the tube at Green Park, across from the Ritz, and walked alongside black cabs and buses to Old Bond Street, celestial with little white lights.

"It's pretty," I said.

"Have you ever seen Paris at Christmastime?"

"I've never been to Paris."

"Never?"

"I told you, we never went on holiday. But maybe you can show me."

She looped an arm through mine. "I'd like that, darling."

The day we'd left Oxford, Fiona had encouraged me to bring a dress shirt, a blazer, and my one decent overcoat. It was only now, browsing Valentino, Chanel, and Saint Laurent, that I understood why. Within a few shops, she bought a sweater for her father, offhandedly, as if he were easy to please. It was her mother she seemed concerned about.

When she still wasn't done by lunchtime, we stopped to eat. After lunch, Fiona ran into someone she knew, a fellow in tweed whose foppish hair fell in a perfect wave. He leaned down to offer his cheek, arms laden with bags. From what I could gather, he was a friend from boarding school, now on break from Cambridge.

"Paul, this is Peter," Fiona said.

"Peter and Paul!" he said, managing somehow to extend a hand. "Where're Mark and Luke?"

We stood on the pavement, chatting. Paul was nothing if not pleasant, one of those people so undaunted by the world that he would never think to be anything but nice. What struck me, though, was how quickly Fiona fell in with him, how easily she, too, moved in the world. I had never quite seen it, or hadn't wanted to, and it made me feel cynical, the way my friends had been cynical when Fiona and I first got together.

Afterward, my feelings came out sideways. "You let go of my hand."

"Sorry?"

"You let go of my hand when you saw Paul."

"To say hello!"

"Was he your boyfriend?"

"Please. He never looked at me."

"But you wished he had."

Her eyes sharpened. "Now you're being ridiculous."

Fiona settled on something at the very next store, where purses were sparsely arrayed like artifacts in a museum. The purse she chose seemed plain save for a clasp in the shape of an omega. Nonetheless, it cost £150. Sorry that I had nothing to show for myself, I bought the least expensive thing I could find, an umbrella, claiming it was for Mum, though I knew she'd only be angry at the extravagance.

When I turned to leave, Fiona's eyes were raw and trembling.

"What's the matter?"

She left the store without answering, and I followed with a sense of dread. Outside, she said, "Did you see the shopgirl?"

"What about her?"

"She was so rude! She didn't say a word to you!"

I pictured the girl: pencil skirt, blond updo, cinched lips. I was so relieved that Fiona wasn't angry at me that my fear turned quickly to irritation. She knew that bricks had been thrown through our shopfront window in Stoke. That Ramesh and I had been chased through the streets routinely by boot boys and even boot girls, with their shaved heads and sidelocks. What was a buttoned-up shopgirl next to all that?

I took Fiona in my arms. "Trust me, I've seen worse."

"You shouldn't have to."

It occurred to me that she could have spoken up in the shop, could have promptly returned the purse and vowed never to return, but I felt the surge of her breathing, the angry pulse of her love, and didn't say anything.

———

As soon as we got home, Fiona said, "Be a dear and say hello to Mum. I've got to hide the presents."

I found Mrs. Turner at the dining room table, staring at the garden over a cup of tea, so deep in thought I almost backed away, afraid of disturbing her. But she sensed me, turned, and smiled.

"There you are, Peter. Come sit. Let me get you some tea."

On the table sat a teapot in a knitted cozy, but she rose to put on water, then came back to the table with a teacup and saucer.

"What did you get up to today?"

I didn't want to give Fiona away, so I said we went to lunch. "We ran into a friend of hers. Paul."

For some reason, Mrs. Turner pursed her lips. Until that

moment, I hadn't seen much resemblance between mother and daughter, but suddenly I saw Fiona in the palimpsest of her mother's face.

"Fiona tells me you're reading accounting."

"Yes. To help my parents. Partly."

She paused, as if she'd run out of things to say, or as if she had plenty to say but couldn't decide where to start. "What was it like growing up? In catering, I mean."

Some of my earliest and fondest memories, I said, were of working alongside my parents, peeling shrimp and snapping bean sprouts until my fingertips were pruned, but as I got older, the work began to chafe. I wanted to do what other kids got to do: go to the cinema, go on holiday, muck about. "One day when I was twelve or thirteen, I decided I'd had enough. I stayed upstairs and watched telly instead. But I couldn't enjoy it, not with Mum and Dad banging about downstairs. I could hear them having a row, too, so I went back down just to keep the peace. In the end, it was easier to do my part. To be the kind of son they wanted."

Mrs. Turner absorbed this. "You haven't had it easy, have you?"

I was encouraged. We were getting somewhere, the way she was taking an interest, seeing other sides of me. "I suppose not. That's one reason Fiona and I get on," I said, thinking of her years in boarding school. "She hasn't had it easy, either."

Mrs. Turner reared back. "Don't listen to Fiona. She had a perfectly lovely childhood and only the best education."

Before I knew what to say, the kettle whistled, and Fiona came in crying, "Mummy!"

———

Fiona and I were going to dinner alone. "You don't want a couple of old fogeys tagging along," Mr. Turner said when he got home, and I took this for the gesture it was. As Fiona got ready, I waited in one of the reception rooms, perusing pictures of her at the awkward ages—glasses, braces, mushroom haircuts—which brought back snatches of a Larkin poem I'd read in grammar school:

> *Too much confectionery, too rich:*
> *I choke on such nutritious images.*

Not surprisingly, Fiona chose a French restaurant, a *bouchon* in South Kensington with tightly packed wooden tables and walls full of copper pans and bric-a-brac. "I think you'll like *tête de veau*," she said over the menu. "Calf's head." She had pinned her hair in a barrette, which made her ears look elfin. By the wavering light of the votive, she looked thin-lipped and shy, and very much the person I wanted to be with.

The meal began with an entrée of three salads and ended with cheese and *pruneaux au vin*. Toward the end, Fiona said rather anxiously, "We only have two terms left."

I sensed the subject she was trying to broach, one I'd been hoping to broach myself, even before she asked, "What are your plans afterward?"

"I'd love to move to London—"

"So would I," she said, and we looked at each other happily.

"What do you think you'll do?"

"The only thing one *can* do with French—become a governess."

I laughed. "I guess I don't have much choice, either. And I'll still have to help my parents."

"Of course. You can do the books from anywhere."

"No, what I mean is, I'll still have to help in the shop."

She gave me that little moue of hers. She had never liked the fact that I went home once a month to help with the weekend rush.

"Even after you're working in London?"

"You'd be surprised how many Chinese leave London at the weekend to help in takeaways."

"Can't they hire someone?"

"They could. But they don't make much as it is."

She paused, measuring her words. "You'd make more than enough to hire someone yourself."

At that moment, I realized there were two kinds of people in the world: those for whom family meant leisure and those for whom family meant work.

"Remember, my parents don't speak English."

Fiona kinked her brows. "They don't?"

Perhaps I'd kept this to myself. Nonetheless, her innocence vexed me. "Have you ever heard me speaking English on the phone?"

She scowled. "That's no reason to assume. They run a takeaway."

"They cope, yes. But people are always taking the piss out of them. That's why I'm at the front of the shop. And why I go home."

Fiona's eyes fell.

"Look," I said gently, "my parents never taught me how to cook. Never let me near the woks, even when I begged them. Trust me, they don't want that life for me. They just have to hang on for a few more years."

She considered, then shook her head at herself.

"Of course, darling. I'm sorry."

———

By the time we left the restaurant, rain and fog had descended. We hurried to the station hand in hand, to the wet sizzle of traffic, the world dark and shimmering.

After the cold and wet, their villa felt warm and inviting. Getting ready for bed, I thought of my parents, who would work late, then pop a tape into the video. It was what they lived for, it seemed, a little Chinese telly at the end of the night. Whenever their friends went back to Hong Kong, my parents would ask them to tape the latest hit serial on TVB.

Their favorite was *Seung Hoi Tan* or *The Bund*, about gang-sters in 1920s Shanghai and starring a baby-faced Chow Yun-fat. I could picture Dad sitting in his sweat-stained BVDs, rubbing Tiger Balm into his shoulders until the whole place reeked of menthol. Suddenly I was sorry I had asked Fiona to come.

I went downstairs to say good night. A light was on in the study, but I ignored it, drawn by women's voices on the lower ground floor. Halfway down, I heard one voice rise and the other rise to meet it. Instinct told me to turn around. Instead, I kept going, drawn by morbid curiosity. The door to the lower ground floor was closed. It wasn't until I was nearly outside that I heard Mrs. Turner say, "—even if it isn't Hampstead." Suddenly I was sure Mr. Turner would emerge from his study. I hurried back upstairs.

I lay in bed, heart skidding. It sounded like mother and daughter had been arguing about the past, the kind of life Fiona had had, but even then, I sensed it had to do with me.

In time, Fiona appeared. Without a word, she got into bed and held me.

"Everything all right?"

"Everything's fine. Why?" Without waiting for an an-swer, she said, "Let's get some sleep. I still want to show you the heath in the morning."

I didn't press her, just glad to have her close. Whatever the tide, Fiona would protect me.

———

Mum and Dad worked seven nights a week and served lunch every day except Tuesdays and Sundays. Today should have been a lie-in day, but they were getting up early to cook for Fiona. Our plan was to see the heath, catch the mid-morning train, and be in Stoke by noon.

We got up to trickling gray light. The need to whisper and tiptoe made the hour seem even earlier. On Haverstock Hill, bakeries and coffee shops were stirring, their windows burning brightly through the gloom. In one, a woman was wiping a table like someone out of Vermeer, and I wished we weren't in a hurry, that we could sit down and take in the morning. It was something of a strange errand, going to the heath first thing, but Fiona had always loved the ancient tract, its unbroken view, and wanted me to see it.

After rounding the Free Hospital, we took Pond Street to South End Road, past a row of bookshops, charity shops, and chemists. Fiona was in a queer mood, not exactly distant but not exactly talkative, either. It was the peaceable but still-delicate air of people who'd made up after a row. Only we hadn't rowed.

When we came to the edge of the heath, Fiona waved at the next street over. "We don't have time, but Keats House is just over there."

I'd read my share of Keats in grammar school. He wasn't my favorite—Larkin was—but I'd learned some things nonetheless. "When Keats fell in love with Fanny Brawne, her mother disapproved," I said. "But eventually she came round."

I thought Fiona would laugh. Instead, she turned to me, stricken. Then she started up Parliament Hill, past red-brick houses trimmed in white, and I followed doggedly, breath pluming. At the entrance to the heath, pavement gave way to a footpath. Without stopping, she took the path through open fields, the grass still white with hoarfrost. Six months earlier, we'd gone walking in Christ Church Meadow, the spires of Oxford jutting in the distance. Cattle had lolled in the fields, their strange horns curled like pincers. Fiona and I had just been together for the first time, and high-stepping through the meadow, we couldn't stop grinning. How long ago that seemed.

At last we came to the top of the hill, and there she was, the great city herself, downy with fog, which made us seem much higher than we were. As we sat on a bench catching our breath, the hillside empty save for the two of us, I thought of all those since Ethelred the Unready who had conquered this view and all those who had yet to or never would, like my grandfather, who had been surprised to find a long-established Chinese community in Liverpool, seafarers mostly, like him, some of whom had taken up with locals, poor English, Irish, and Welsh girls who then became a kind of scourge, even to their own families, and I knew that time was not a line or an arc but a sine, a wave, forever vacillating.

"You aren't coming to Stoke, are you?"

For a long moment, Fiona squinted fiercely into the distance. Then she pressed her forehead to my shoulder, and I felt ashamed that my first feeling was relief.

"And we'll never see Paris, will we?"

She wrapped her arms around me, the cold wedge of her nose buried in my neck, and I saw it all: the long walk back to the house, the longer train ride home, the baffled looks of my parents. And I knew how I would spend my last two terms: in orbit, far from the center of town, or in a study carrel at the Bodleian, where despite the rules, the threat to the precious past, I would cup my tiny flame.

Allhallows

THE DAY BEFORE HALLOWEEN, ERNIE STOOD IN THE MEN'S room relieving himself on break. That's when the clammy, gray face of Troy Festerling, grill master, loomed into view. Troy belonged to that breed of men who liked to banter over the partition, like neighbors over a fence. Favorite subject: the "snatch" in the chow line. Ernie kept his eyes on the urinal screen and its built-in cake of deodorant.

"Ernest."

"What?"

"Ernmeister."

Despite himself, Ernie looked up to see Troy's face listing toward his with a crooked grin. "I said, 'What?'"

"Want to make some dough?"

Ernie bristled. He had mentioned struggling with

alimony only once, in a rare moment of candor, yet here Troy was, exploiting the knowledge.

"How?"

"Special delivery."

Ernie knew enough to know exactly what needed delivering. The only thing that kept him from dismissing the idea out of hand was asking where and recognizing the small town on the coast where the delivery was to be made. Their first year here, he and his then-wife had driven down with the boys the day after Thanksgiving to watch Santa Claus sail in on a shrimp boat. They had stayed at a charming inn topped by a widow's walk and cupola, and each night after the boys went down they'd sat in rocking chairs and nursed bourbons on the wraparound porch, relishing the newfound wonders of the South, during what might have been their last best time. Those memories gave the overture an air of possibility. That and the money.

"Why don't you do it yourself?"

"Car troubles," Troy replied, the answer ready-made.

"Are you trying to get me killed?"

Troy cocked another grin. "Maybe."

For the rest of the day neither broached the subject. Then Troy reared up again and said, "Okay, man, you win. I'll throw in another hundred—and all of it up front." He handed over three grainy new hundred-dollar bills. "And there's more where that came from."

At midnight, back at the college, their two cars side by side in an otherwise empty parking lot, Troy produced an enormous purple teddy bear, the kind dispensed at mid-ways for the most dexterous of feats, like ringing a bottle or shooting out a star. "Just sit him right up front," he said, shoving the bear in.

An hour later, Ernie was on the road, driving past inflat-able churches and hand-painted signs for boiled peanuts. Even after three years, the novelty of the South still struck him. He had grown up in Manhattan at the corner of East Broadway and Market Street, where his father ran a Hung Gar school. If his father had had his way it would have been the Wan Ming Lee & Son Hung Gar School, but Ernie never took to kung fu; instead, he played hockey. Became a goalie in Pee Wee. Almost made the National Under-17 team. Dreamed like his buddies of the NHL. Larry "China Clipper" Kwong had played for Ernie's beloved Rangers back in 1948—ten whole years before Willie O'Ree, the Jackie Robinson of hockey!— but only for a minute in the third period in his one and only game, which seemed a technical first. Ernie wanted to be the first Chinese *star*. If his parents had indulged him, it was only because the Ivy League had hockey teams, too. But when his grades fell short, he opted for St. Cloud State in Minnesota, a Division III school with a Division I hockey program. "Herb Brooks coached there," he enthused. "You know, Miracle on Ice." His parents blinked uncertainly for all they would never understand.

After college, he'd signed a two-way contract with Van-couver and for one golden summer he seemed on his way. But outside of training camp every September, he never played on the West Coast. Instead, he toiled for the minor league affiliate in Syracuse, where his form steadily eroded. Four years later, he signed with the Tallahassee Tiger Sharks of the third tier East Coast Hockey League in a last-ditch effort to salvage his career, which explained how he came to be in the South and in a car hurtling toward the Gulf of Mexico with a drug-filled carnival prize riding shotgun.

After winding along the coast for nearly an hour, eyes on the speedometer, he came to a small oystering town on the far side of a darkened bay. As he sat in the car facing the very dock where Santa had alighted, he kept telling himself he was safe, that no one could possibly know, that the world remained as blind as ever to the things roiling about inside him. At the appointed hour, a figure, a man, appeared on the dock. Calmly, breathlessly, Ernie walked over and proffered the bear, to no surprise, and just like that he was done, released. After circling the town once, he sped home ecstatically. With no time to sleep and too wired besides, he downed a pot of coffee and went to work, relaying success to Troy through only the curtest of nods. By the time he got home, he'd been up for a day and a half. Hours later he awoke to a feeling of pleasure, for his triumph and the kingly rest that had followed. What he would never tell his ex-wife: he hadn't overslept his plans to take the boys for Halloween; he had forgotten them altogether.

———

Every other week in Tallahassee, a giant mechanical talon came around to pick up oversized garbage, which meant every other week the streets were strewn with ugly armchairs, grubby mattresses, mangled swing sets, and rusty water heaters. This was the scene that greeted him as he turned into his old neighborhood just north of Frenchtown. He stopped in front of a house with a faux brick wainscot and a sun-peeled metal awning. Christa had rules about showing up unannounced, but he wanted to see the boys, make it up to them somehow. If he had called, she would have been done with him on the phone.

As he started up the walk, the front door opened and Ben, his older boy, appeared on the threshold. "Dad, where were you?" he cried. He raced down the steps, then stopped abruptly, checking himself. Ernie crouched, arms wide. In an overflow of relief, Ben ran the rest of the way and slung his head over his father's shoulder.

Ernie squeezed his son with the feeling of being watched, a feeling he had always had as a parent but all the more so since getting divorced. Now that he only saw Christa passing the kids back and forth, he found himself performing, overacting, to prove in those fleeting moments of contact his ability to father.

But when he looked up, she wasn't there blocking the doorway, which seemed a good sign, a virtual invitation, so he poked his head in the door. Toby, his four-year-old, was playing with cars on the living room floor. On the other side of the kitchen peninsula, his wife—his ex-wife—stood in profile at the sink, lost in the sound of running water.

"Hey, Toby," he whispered.

Toby looked up serenely, then went back to his cars—reproof, it seemed, for last night. Then again, the boy had always been remote, like his mother, especially after the accident that had left him half-blind in one eye.

"Mom, Dad's here!" Ben shouted.

Christa turned and smiled absentmindedly. Then she looked up and her smile dissolved. Last night she'd left two messages on his machine. The first: "You've got to be kidding, Ernie." The second: "I'm starting to get worried. Call me when you get this." He'd left a message at the office where she temped, hoping a night of worry might expand to regret, even love. But whatever she had felt last night was gone.

She shut off the water, then rounded the counter with a tea towel in her hands. She was still dressed for work in a shimmery blouse with a bow collar, her blond hair up in a loose bun, and the air of naughty secretary made him wince inwardly. He didn't like the thought of her out in the world looking better than she had at nineteen.

"So. What happened?".

When he'd first proposed Halloween, she'd said "That might be doable" and left it at that. He could have accused her of ambiguity but didn't. Instead, he lied. Long shifts at work, compounding exhaustion, a mishap with the alarm. "I'm sorry, Ben, Tobes."

Christa studied him. Then she walked over, arms raised.

Her first hug in months, and surprisingly tender. Maybe a night of lying awake had indeed dredged up old feelings.

He rubbed his hands together happily, theatrically. "So how much candy did you get?"

"We didn't get *any* candy!"

"How come?"

"We didn't go trick-or-treating."

"What do you mean you didn't go?" He turned to Christa accusingly.

"They wouldn't go," she replied calmly. "They wanted you. Fell asleep waiting."

"Don't worry, Dad. Mom bought candy."

"Well, that's not the same, is it?" His plan had been to extract the boys for ice cream, but now he had a new plan. "Go put on your costumes."

Toby looked up, his milky eye darting.

"Ernie."

"Why not?" he asked, strangely pleased with himself.

Now the boys were on his side, clamoring.

"Just a few houses," he said. "Just to say we did." He expected a glare but she seemed unusually composed.

"All right," she said. "Wait here. We'll just be a minute."

As she helped the boys get ready, he thought about her sudden embrace. Back in college, after months of seeming indifference, she'd snuck up on him at a party and squeezed his arm in passing, and the world had opened up, and though she would grant much more on her skinny single in Shoemaker Hall, and in the room where she'd slept as a child on a dauntingly quiet street in Eau Claire, and in the lakeside cottage in the Dells where he had proposed, he still thought of that fleeting exchange as the most intimate moment of their courtship. Maybe today was another opening.

The boys came running out, Ben in a red nose and a rainbow wig. "Dad, what do you think?"

"A clown and a monkey?"

"It's what they wanted."

"What's wrong? Don't you like it?"

"Like it? I love it. My sons, Bozo and Bubbles."

Christa didn't flinch. Instead, she hustled the boys to the door. "Have fun," she said. "Don't be long."

———

He decided to take the boys a ways, far from immediate neighbors. As the three of them pushed along, Ben looking up to keep his big red nose from slipping, Ernie imagined people would think they'd been out all night and then some, wandering the wilderness for candy.

Eventually they heard a voice: "Y'all are a little late, aren't you?"

Across the street, a co-ed out on her porch stared from under the bill of her cap. She sat low in her chair with her feet up, a glass of something in her hand. Ernie stepped to the curb, hands in pockets, squinting in a hangdog way. Through no fault of their own, the boys had missed Halloween, he explained. "Any chance you have something left over?"

She took a sip of her drink, considering. Then she set down her feet, first one, then the other, languorously. "Let me see what we got."

As the girl slipped inside, Ernie caught sight of her legs and her tiny cut-off jeans and felt something inside him lurch. Since moving out at the start of the year, he hadn't been with anyone. If he had, if he were to, Christa would never take him back. To have any hope at all, he would have to be a saint. But at least she wasn't dating, either. She had always been haughty and gun-shy and would only be more so now. Plus, she had the boys. It wasn't just that most men were wary of kids; it was the fact that his kids would always betray a different father, and he liked this, the thought of his genes fighting the good fight, warding off southern boys.

They crossed the street expectantly, but when the girl came back she said, "Sorry, we don't have anything left. My boyfriend must have ate it all." She rose prettily on her toes and pointed. "Try over there. They had candy last night."

But they had no luck there, either. As the boys came trudging back, Ben hanging his head, Toby swinging his bag like a scythe, Ernie felt a creep of doubt. Maybe Christa was right. Maybe this was a bad idea. He thought about taking the boys home but loathed the thought of going back empty-handed. Something in Christa had changed; the long-awaited thaw had begun. If only he could rustle up half a bag of candy, the ice might finally break.

To change their luck, they went a block over. There they came to a house with a curdling pumpkin outside, which seemed a safe bet. But the craggy-faced man who came to the door did not exude an air of festivity. When the boys shouted in unison, he sniffed the air, spotted Ernie, shot him a look. "What's the idea?"

Ernie smiled. "Sorry to bother you, sir. These are my boys, Ben and Toby. Their mother didn't take them out last night, if you can believe it." Which was true, and cause for a little fraternizing, he hoped. "We saw your pumpkin and thought you might have something left over."

The man eyed the gourd resentfully, trying to decide how much it obliged him. Without a word, he vanished inside. Ben turned to his father. Ernie gave him the thumbs-up.

The man returned with a wooden bowl and lowered it without stooping. As the boys dithered, he stared at them in a way that Ernie had come to recognize and disliked. He often wished he could take the boys back to New York or maybe out to California, somewhere people didn't think twice about halfers. He kept urging Christa to move, but she said she liked the South just fine.

"Quickly now, boys."

Things picked up from there. People were surprised but good-natured. Of those who no longer had candy, one gave apples and another brandished a little toy guillotine whose small white blade passed *right through* their fingers. Toby grinned maniacally and Ernie imagined the day enshrining itself in family lore. "Hey, Dad, remember the time . . ." Toby would ask, a grown man himself, regaled by the memory.

Eventually they came to a house where a woman was

waiting for them on the steps. She wore a gray sweatsuit and her hair was restrained in two ways, in a ponytail *and* a thin plastic headband, and in her lap she held a pumpkin-shaped bucket. "Happy Halloween! Great costumes!" she said with no less affect than she must have had last night.

"Thank you, ma'am. We really appreciate it."

For some reason, her eyes welled faintly. "You came to the right place. Candy is something we got, let me tell you." She laughed bitterly, at her own expense, it seemed. Something to do with her weight maybe—a tad on the plus side.

As the boys peered into the bucket, she said, "Haven't seen you in a while."

When Ernie pinched his brows, she made running motions with her arms.

"Oh, right." He had the sudden image of her sitting at her window waiting for him to jog past. Apparently watching the street was something she did.

"You quit?"

"No, I just—run at the gym now."

"I was gonna say. You look in shape to me."

At that moment, lumbering footsteps came from somewhere inside and a boy—ruddy, heavyset, close-cropped—appeared in the doorway. He threw his head back and roared. "What are you guys, retarded?"

The woman snapped her head to one side. "Grady Jefferson. You take that back right now."

The boy laughed.

"Then no more Xbox today."

"Aw."

"Well?"

After a long moment, the boy said, "Hey, you guys wanna play Xbox?"

A few pounds of pressure left the woman's body. "That's nice of you, Grady. But I think they better ask their daddy."

Ben and Toby turned to him, so eagerly that he made a mental note to buy them an Xbox for Christmas. Now he had the money.

"Hate to intrude."

The woman pshawed. "Let them have fun."

He heard Christa warning him not to be long, but he liked the idea of ending on a high note. "One game," he said, holding up a stern finger. The boys leaped onto the porch. Grady bounced on the threshold, caught up in the excitement. "Come on, you Japanese freaks!"

"Grady!" the woman cried, but the boys were already gone. She buried her face in her hands, then drew up, slapping her knees.

Ernie said, "Kids."

She smiled gratefully. "Want to wait inside?"

"Sure. Why not?"

The house had the feel of a rental: futon, floor lamp, papasan chair. From all the graven images of Chief Osceola, it was clear where the woman had gone to school or at least where her football loyalties lay.

"What street are you on again?"

"Actually, I don't live around here anymore. But their mother still does."

"Ohhh," she said. "What'd you do, mess around?"

He barked a laugh. "Do I look like the type?"

She scrunched her eyes. "You're a man, aren't you?"

The woman had taken the futon, which left Ernie with the papasan. He tried to sit up but soon flung himself back as if floating on an inner tube.

"Nope, never."

"What was it, then? God, I'm being nosy, aren't I?"

Somehow he didn't mind. After his last season with the Tiger Sharks, the franchise moved, which meant all the guys and their network of wives and girlfriends simply decamped. He wondered if this sudden aloneness hadn't hastened the end of his marriage. In any case, it meant he hadn't had anyone to talk to.

Their troubles had had something to do with money, especially compared to their friends who had made it to the bigs, but Christa had also accused him of being a mediocre father—*disinterested* was the word. The accusation had jolted him, so far was her view from his view of himself, but he knew there was some truth to it. His problems never vanished around the boys; he could still dwell abstractedly on a bad goal, a bad game, a bad season. And he was always a little relieved to be on the road. Days or weeks without diapers or tantrums, just hockey, poker, restaurants, and a soundly sleeping roommate.

"Guess I was something of a lousy father."

The woman raised a brow. "Really? Grady would be lucky if his daddy *ever* came around."

She launched into the story of her ex-husband, whom she referred to as Rat Bastard. They'd been high school sweethearts in Valdosta, Georgia, went to school together at Florida State, as he might have guessed—she looked around and laughed—got married after graduation, had a baby soon thereafter. Then she caught him messing around. Now he lived in Jacksonville with his new family, rich as sin from some Internet venture. "Lord knows I love Grady," she said, "but I can't stand that he's half Rat Bastard."

Ernie wondered if Christa had a nasty little name for him.

The woman sighed. "I need a drink. Want one?"

"I should probably check on the boys."

"I'll do that. You stay here."

She came back with a beer in each hand. "Don't worry. They're having a ball."

She sat back down, took a swig, and picked some lint off her thigh. "Do I really look that old?"

His bottle came off his lips with an airy pop. "I'm sorry?"

"You ma'amed me. I hate it when guys do that."

The welling in her eyes—now he understood. But he hadn't meant anything by it. In fact, she was halfway good-looking. A bit on the chunky side, but now that her hoodie was open he saw how easily she filled her tank top.

"Sorry. Just reflex."

Still picking lint, she asked, "What happened to the little one's eye?"

The question made his heart start. He supposed it all began with the move to Tallahassee and the ECHL, which meant riding the bus to towns like Jackson, Mississippi, and North Little Rock, Arkansas, places anathema to hockey. He had grown up dreaming of donning the noble shield of the Rangers and squaring off against the winged P of the Flyers, the spoked B of the Bruins. Instead, he wound up facing a cartoon nightmare of Sea Wolves, Ice Pilots, and Lizard Kings, even a team called the Grrrowl. Then the topper: the Tiger Sharks announced they were moving to Macon, Georgia, and becoming the Whoopee. The Apocalypse was upon him.

So he retired. Or rather, fizzled into anonymity, which meant a regular job for the first time in his life. On the morning of his first interview, he drove to a used-car dealership on the parkway. The owner was a sports fan, memorabilia all over. He recognized Ernie, thought his minor celebrity might be worth a few sales, and Ernie felt his hockey career paying its final dividends. Afterward, when he turned on his phone, he was jarred by all the missed calls. Half a message later, he was racing to Tallahassee Memorial.

When he finally found Christa, she turned to him in a cool fury. "The iron. You didn't put it back." By *back* she meant in its metal holder, the one she had bought at a Scandinavian box store and screwed to the wall herself. A sickening wave swept over him, even as he remembered slamming the iron into place. But maybe he had altered the memory in the act of wishing.

In the weeks and months that followed, Ernie learned

more about the eye than he ever cared to know. Operation followed upon operation, some requiring Toby to stay im- mobilized afterward for impossible stretches at a time. Yet those days now seemed halcyon, all those hours of reading to him and keeping up his spirits, for as soon as he was up and about, Christa said, "I'd like you to go."

Between gulps of beer, he recounted the bare minimum, suddenly annoyed that his audience was this somewhat ri- diculous woman, insecure and overweight and obsessed with her ex-husband—

And that's when it came to him: Christa was in love. Christa was in love, only not with him. That's why she wasn't going to move. Out of guilt or one of her hang-ups, she'd been moving at a glacial pace, maybe for months and months, but she wouldn't have to now that she thought Ernie had finally moved on. What else would she think after he'd been out all night? That or at home refusing to answer her calls? When she asked him what had happened, it was with hope, and when he lied, she could tell, she could always tell. So she gave him one last hug as spiritual man and wife to say, *Good for you, Ernie. You've found someone. Now we're both free. Our cove- nant is broken forever and ever.*

He didn't see the woman approach until her hand was in his hair. "Poor baby," she said. "You poor, poor baby." She tried to climb into the papasan, only to slide right into him. Suddenly her face was next to his and the watery weight of her breasts against him. Her eyes welled again, this time entreatingly, and it seemed a little of the world's bounty had at last trickled down to him. He closed his eyes and let the inevitable happen, and for a moment it seemed he was young again, his body still new, unspent, and huddled under covers in residence at Shoemaker Hall as snow fell long into the night.

———

He was roused by the sound of a door slamming. In his addled state, he thought Rat Bastard had come home. Then he recalled that the man lived three hours away and couldn't give a damn. The woman was smiling in her sleep, arms winged from under her face, and for a moment he almost felt tender. Then he remembered the boys.

He dressed quickly. As he slipped out of the bedroom and down the hall—without running into Grady, thankfully—he wondered how he had managed to sleep with a woman whose name he didn't know, without protection, and whether in doing so he had tied his sons forever to that asshole of a kid. Whether he was twice bound to a city he had never imagined living in.

He hurried back to Christa's, hoping to intercept the boys, but a block away from the house he found Ben's red nose on the sidewalk. The boys had beat him.

He stood outside the house waiting for someone to come to the window. That's where the boys appeared every Sunday, waving as he left. No such luck today, but he couldn't bring himself to leave, the way he couldn't quite leave that small town on the Gulf Coast two nights earlier when he'd stopped outside the inn and stared at the windows, trying to recall which room had been theirs. Looking up at the widow's walk, he had imagined himself the mariner and Christa the wife looking out to sea. He used to think it was enough that he came back every time, faithfully. It never occurred to him just how lonely a life she must have led.

He turned to go. Stepping toward the car, he spotted a cardboard box at the curb, one flap marked with the word FREE, Christa's modest contribution to the flotsam and jetsam of the neighborhood. Inside he saw a few things he recognized: a frying pan, a cutting board, a tea kettle. At the bottom he spied two pieces of plastic, one green and one gold. Once, years ago in Syracuse, when Ben was still a baby, Christa had sent him out for teething gel. A wintry night, lake-effect snow, and so cold that the aisles of the CVS seemed a veritable hearth. In the baby aisle, he'd come upon a pair of water-filled teethers, one in the shape of a frog and the other in the shape of a goldfish. Imagining the comfort they would bring, he'd bought them along with the gel. Driving home, he'd been proud of himself, of his two-pronged ingenuity, but when he got home Christa told him they were made of the wrong plastic, and they were quickly whisked to the bottom of a drawer. Now he picked them up and slipped them into his pocket with a searing feeling of relief, to think that his mistakes might have no cost.

We Two Alone

AT THE START OF THE FINAL SCENE, IN THE MIDDLE OF HIS speech to Cordelia, Leonard's mind went blank. One moment his mind was full and the next it was empty, like a lake instantly drained, and the feeling was eerie. He scoured his memory, expecting words to leap to his tongue, to rush back in, but none came. Suddenly the stage lights prickled and his costume weighed like a lead apron.

Leonard Xiao had waited a decade to play Lear. As the founder, director, and lead actor of the Asian American Shakespeare Company, he alone decided what got put on every year. At a hale-looking forty-eight, he was still too young for the role, but this was the company's tenth year, which called for a play with commemorative heft.

Leonard had always been known for his memory. Just last year, playing Henry V, he'd been flawless, even in rehearsal.

Famously, he never needed scripts for table work, just recited entire plays by heart. But this year was different. At the table read, he found himself stumbling, using the prompt book. In rehearsal, he snapped impatiently for cues. He and Emily had separated after twenty years, and the strain was taking its toll. He thought *Lear* would finally bring her out of obscurity, but she hadn't shown up for last night's opening and he hadn't seen her tonight, either. His mind was addled.

But he feared it wasn't that, or not just that. Before she died, his mother had lost her memory. What had surprised him about her decline was not the forgetting so much as the darkening of her mood, the sudden, improbable fits of rage. Once, when his parents were in town, he took them to a Japanese restaurant, a little hole-in-the-wall in the Bowery. After he asked for a table, his mother decided she wanted to go somewhere else. When he said they ought to stay—the waitress had already set down menus—his mother began to yell, to hurl insults, until he and his father had no choice but to whisk her out. Now that same darkness was seeping into him. The first time they rehearsed the final act of *Lear*, the young man who played the Captain, whose small but vital role was to show a range of feeling as Edmund orders Lear and Cordelia to be executed—the young man had put on such a ridiculous pantomime that Leonard had lost it. "Who are you? Marcel fucking Marceau?" The young man had cowered in shame, the outburst so unlikely that Leonard had surprised even himself.

When all this evidence began to mount, all he wanted

was to make it through the run without going up on a line. When he made it through opening night he was buoyed, and until a moment ago, a second clean performance had seemed within reach. But now he was looking at Sophie Hsu—Cordelia—baffled as to what came next. They were holding hands, and he felt a clasp of assurance, even as her eyes quickened from worry to pity to panic. As he turned to the shrouded darkness of the house, a tiny rental on West 45th Street, he had time to think that her stricken looks could be read as Cordelia's and his own befuddled ones as Lear's. He kept rooting around for the rest of the line, patting the high shelf in his mind where he swore he had left it. Nothing.

Just as silence threatened to unnerve the audience, Edmund stepped forward and said, "Take them away," and everything else came rushing back.

Afterward, Leonard passed Ryan Gushiken backstage. As soon as Ryan had rescued the moment, the lost lines had resurfaced. Only those thoroughly versed in the play would have missed them, and even then, they might have been taken for deliberate excisions. So Ryan hadn't been wrong to cover. But Leonard could tell he expected thanks, with his usual air of conceit, all the more galling for having a basis in talent. Always these young Turks trying to show him up. He walked on.

Later, outside the dressing rooms, Leonard ran into Sophie, who appeared to be waiting.

"Wow, that was close," she said, trying to forge intimacy

out of near disaster. When he said nothing, she glanced off, then snuck a look. "Want to go for a drink?"

Sophie was a slender, open-faced girl from Saratoga Springs, seduced by her first stint in the city. Throughout rehearsals, he had felt an honest affection for her, this girl who was indeed young enough to be his daughter.

"Didn't we have enough last night?" he asked, thinking of all the drinks he had bought for the cast and crew as well as his father, who had come, however torpidly, for opening night. "Maybe that's what did me in."

"Just one, then."

There had been a time when a nightcap and whatever else with a fresh-faced ingénue would have been precisely the thing, but all he could think of now was Emily.

"Sorry, can't. Not tonight."

Her eyes glazed with hurt.

"Some other time."

"Okay," she sniffed. "Some other time."

———

Losing his mind to *Lear*. What a fucking cliché.

This was the thought that possessed him as he rumbled through sweaty catacombs all the way up to Washington Heights. There were five more shows to get through in the weeklong run, so he riffled through his lines, more than seven hundred, but as far as he could tell they were all still there, including the ones he'd forgotten, and it struck him anew, the sheer sorcery of memory. By the time he reached his apartment, he felt better. Maybe he *was* stressed. Maybe it *was* the drinking. Even if he was destined to become his mother, he should have had another decade. So maybe he wasn't losing his mind just yet.

After dropping his keys in the bowl by the door, he sat in the dark, taking in his narrow slice of the river. For years, he and Emily had let one of the itinerant actors crash on their couch for the show's duration, but this year, without Emily to play house mom, he couldn't be bothered. Without the usual company, he felt her absence all the more. Six months ago, in this very room, the two of them had staged their own final scene. She was done, she said. Done with the city, done with the dream. She was forty-two years old. If it hadn't happened by now, it was never going to happen. It wasn't a question of talent, whether she had it or not; some element of timing or karma or grace had passed her by, and she was tired, sick and tired of everything.

It wasn't that Leonard couldn't understand. He was just as tired of cattle calls, bit parts, standby, rejection. Tired of his father, a physicist at Harvard, asking, "So where's your Oscar?" But he couldn't bring himself to quit, now that the company had a toehold in the city. Sooner or later, someone would see him, and everything would come to pass. The late bloom—it was still possible.

"Why can't you let it go?" she asked.

Sometimes he wanted to. He could easily imagine the pleasures of a regular job and a regular paycheck, a healthy balance in his 401(k) and evenings and weekends to himself. As a teenager, he had whiled away entire weekends just watching TV and napping, and he longed to be that free again from the exigence of time, the constant need to make use of it, and the feeling of running out. But walking away would mean his life had been a mistake, and he wasn't ready to admit that.

But she was. By saying she wanted to quit, wanted *them* to quit, she was saying she no longer believed. In either of them.

He sat in the glow of his phone, scrolling. For the past six months, neither he nor Emily had been active on social media. He kept up with posts about the show, but that was about it. Anyone paying attention would have noticed their absence, the sudden ghosting of their life as a couple. Emily had posted only twice, once about a cat with feline leukemia and once about a sandwich she was having at Eisenberg's (with whom? he had wondered). She had never been one to parade her private life in public. If she was seeing someone, which wasn't beyond the realm of possibility, she wouldn't post or tweet about it, not without telling him first, but he didn't put it past someone else to tag her on a date. So he checked his feeds. Tonight, once again, nothing.

———

They met the year he moved to L.A. He was sitting in the waiting room of a little theater when the casting assistant called his name. When Leonard stood, the CA looked at his clipboard and said, "You'll be reading with Emily Gardner." The first thing Leonard noticed was her bowl cut. He knew what she was going for, something punky and boyish, but her hair had been lopped off in a way that almost seemed rude. Still, he could tell she was pretty. But pretty wasn't what he needed. What he needed was someone who could act.

After a postgrad year in London, he had flown straight from Heathrow to LAX, eager to make up for lost time, those wasted years between degrees when he'd followed the straight and narrow, trying to please his father. His father hadn't been happy about London or the fact that Leonard hadn't bothered to stop in Cambridge— Cambridge, Massachusetts—before venturing west, but the way Leonard saw it, the sooner he found success, the sooner he would smooth things over at home.

He shook Emily's hand, said hello—the normal, decent thing to do, but also a stab at rapport. It never helped to go on cold. "You ready for this?"

"I think so." Her voice was small and warbling.

"Have you done this before?"

"Of course," she said, a little testy.

The casting assistant led them out. They had only a moment as they walked to the stage to go over the scene, compare notes, which they did under their breath, as if cheating on a test. Onstage, they stood before a dark curtain. When the director gave the signal, Emily closed her eyes and kept them closed. Leonard couldn't tell if she was already in character or summoning the courage to start—or worse, trying to remember her line. His heart withered.

Then it happened: she opened her eyes, started to speak, and morphed into someone else, voice sharp and stringent. He'd seen this kind of transformation before, but it didn't make hers any less surprising. Just a few lines and he knew: she had the stuff, and his confidence surged. They were playing a young married couple. She was a drunk and he was a sop and they were having it out. By turns simpering, mawkish, and prosecutorial, she tried to extract a confession that he was sleeping with someone else. He could feel the scene working, the two of *them* working. It was already there: the trust, the chemistry.

"You were really good," he said when they stepped out into the parking lot.

"You think so?" she asked, demure again.

"*Really* good."

"So were you."

Neither would get a part, but in that moment, it seemed like they might, and they stood by her car in the dusty squall of the parking lot, relishing the possibility. He kept waiting for her to pull out her keys and say, *Well, it was nice to meet you,* but they talked for so long that the actors who must have gone after them, the guy who had bobbed along obnoxiously to the staticky wafts of his headphones and the redhead in the tartan skirt, thigh-highs, and penny loafers who had blown in noisily, hungry for attention—the two of them walked out together, got straight into a car, and drove off, their headlong coupling a kind of indictment, enough for Emily to finally ask, "Want to grab lunch?" and the reel of time got flung out, thrillingly.

———

Emily was raised by her mother alone in a small town outside of Harrisburg, Pennsylvania. Her mother made pendants and brooches out of sea glass and wire, and she sold them on the festival circuit. As a child, Emily had spent many a night on the road in the back of her mother's car, wondering at the moon. In high school, she caught the drama bug and spent weekends bagging groceries at the local Karns to send herself to theater camps. The day she got into Yale was the day her life began.

That's what Leonard learned over lunch, and then, when lunch wasn't time enough, hiking through Solstice Canyon. "Have you seen the ocean yet?" she'd asked. "Only on the flight in," he'd said. "Then we have to go!" They went their separate ways to change, then drove together from her place. As they followed a sun-struck path through sagebrush and chaparral, Emily in shorts and a tank and a pair of serious-looking hiking boots, her pale shoulders slathered an even ghostlier white, they recounted their lives in New Haven and London—the shows they'd been in, the shows they'd seen—and Leonard felt exquisitely happy. To be out, to be free, not holed up running through lines, and to be with someone new and interesting who was willing and eager to hang, which seemed the very definition of fun: someone you liked who made time. In London, Leonard had dated a sweet, high-minded girl on the drama and movement therapy track. They might have made a life for themselves in the city, but she kept talking of moving back to the Midlands and becoming a school-based drama therapist and having kids of her own. She hadn't been keen on the thought of him starring on ITV or Channel 4, much less in Hollywood. But Emily—now here was someone striving, slugging it out as she was among the tens of thousands of would-be stars in L.A., someone who seemed to understand the mania that burned only in actors.

At the end of the Rising Sun Trail, they came to the ruins of a burned-down mansion, just the foundation and a few brick walls. Instead, of turning back, they carried on, took another trail to the Deer Valley Loop. It was here that the ocean reared up colossally, a rimpled expanse of blue that stretched all the way to the bending horizon. It was probably a mile away, but somehow it had never seemed closer. In his excitement, he'd gotten ahead of Emily. He turned and waved, and she waved back, sinuously, her short hair windswept, her green eyes bright and glistening.

———

What he thought of as their final scene wasn't the final scene. Parting wasn't going to be easy, not after twenty years. She couldn't just walk out; she had to come back for her things. She was staying with a friend in Brooklyn, and every few days he would come home to some molecular disturbance in the air and find yet more clothes or books or kitchenware gone. It was almost a game, trying to figure out what had been taken.

A few weeks after leaving, she returned with the friend from Brooklyn in tow. Their coats were dusted with snow and exuded a wintry tang, and her friend could not disguise the mortification of seeing him. Leonard wondered if Emily had always come with Tara or if this marked a new phase of their separation: the taking of things that required more than one person. Tara carried out a framed picture that must have been buried somewhere in the bedroom closet, a circle of rainbow elephants joined nose to tail, and the sight of this half-remembered thing, destined at one time for a nursery, made his throat go raw. Alone with him, Emily said, "You know I don't want this." It wasn't clear what "this" meant, life as it had been or life as it was unfolding, but his heart was still tundra, the thaw not yet begun, so he didn't say anything. After a final, determined sweep, the women repatriated Emily's favorite thing in the world, her Heywood-Wakefield tambour desk, rounded like the edge of an airplane wing.

That was the final scene.

———

Leonard slept poorly, thinking of *Lear*, thinking of Emily. It was one of those nights, too, when the window unit gurgled plangently, every inch of his body skimmed with sweat. For hours, he scudded along the surface of sleep. Then, near daybreak, he fell into that deep valley and couldn't pull himself out.

It was almost noon when he sat down with a cup of coffee and the folio version of *Lear*. To test himself, he read with a piece of paper over his lines. Everyone thought he had a powerful memory, but he didn't. He had to use every trick in the book: writing things out, color-coding. He would even tape his lines and listen at all hours, walking the streets or riding the subway or drifting off to sleep, hoping they would earworm as idly as a pop song. And, of course, he rehearsed.

As he paced the living room, rehearsing still more, he remembered himself as a child, walking in blinkered circles and mouthing multiplication tables. This was back in Chicago, where his father did graduate work in physics after compulsory military service in Taiwan and before his first and only job at Harvard. His father had wanted him to learn the language of the cosmos, but for Leonard numbers had never held much in the way of beauty or mystery. It wasn't until the seventh grade when he was cast as Noah Claypole in the school production of *Oliver!* that he learned to appreciate what his father had taught him. If he was supposed to be good at learning by rote, then he would apply that skill to the one art where it mattered. At twelve, this had seemed deliciously subversive to him.

That night, the third night of *Lear*, after he'd put on the makeup and wig and hoary beard that aged him considerably, Rebecca, the stage manager—Bex, he called her—strode into the dressing room in jeans and a black blazer, her hair dark, curled, and vampirically peaked.

"How 'bout we try one of these tonight?"

She held out her hand. In the divot of her palm sat what looked like an amputated fingertip, complete with flesh tone.

"No."

"Just in case."

"I'm not using an earpiece," he said, stalking out.

Throughout the show, he felt vindicated. He was in command, words burbling up like a spring. If anything, he was preoccupied with looking for Emily. In the early years, the company had lit the house as part of original practice, but most of the actors had found all the uncloaked faces unnerving, so they went back to darkening the house. Now he wished they hadn't.

Emily was still on his mind as he raged against the storm, but when he said, "My wits begin to turn," he thought of himself. Nothing, however, was wrong with him tonight. He was flawless.

"See?" he said to Bex backstage. "Tight as a drum."

On his way out, Sophie reared up again in jeans and a T-shirt, her hair piled up and loosely skewered. "How about that drink?"

Sophie could have been his daughter in another way: she was half Chinese. This gave her face a slippery, quicksilver quality. These days, his players came from all manner of background—Portuguese-Japanese, Dutch-Irish-Malaysian,

Indian-Puerto Rican—which made being Chinese feel almost retrograde.

"Yeah, I don't know."

Her eyes narrowed. "I'm new to the city. Don't you remember what that's like?"

He did, all too well, and he felt for her. But just as he was about to cave, Ryan Gushiken happened past, a muscle in his jaw rippling, and Leonard felt caught, exposed somehow.

"You'll be fine," he said, gripping her shoulder. "See you tomorrow."

———

The year after they met, Leonard and Emily went to the Vista in Los Feliz to see *Fargo*, the new Coen brothers movie. By this point their lives had found a rhythm: auditioning by day, waiting tables by night, then crashing at her place or his. On nights off, they liked going for drinks at Small's on Melrose or listening to music at the Palace on Vine.

The movie began with a whiteout, which brought Leonard back to Chicago, the stupefying winters he had endured there, first as a child and then as an undergraduate. He recognized the loping Midwestern accents, the duplicities of Minnesota nice, and he was enjoying the story, the lunkheadedness of human desperation, when a character named Mike Yanagita appeared. Leonard recognized the actor from *Do the Right Thing* and *In Living Color*, and it gave him hope that he himself was on the verge, that there would soon be a surfeit of roles for the likes of him.

In the movie, Marge Gunderson, the main character, had just arrived at a hotel restaurant, and Mike Yanagita rose from a booth to greet her. Even though Marge was unmistakably pregnant, Mike rolled his eyes lubriciously as he held her too long. After some labored small talk, he tried to slide into the same side of the booth as Marge, only to be rebuffed, and something roiled inside Leonard. Mike went on to explain that his wife, Linda Cooksey, had died of leukemia. Then he happened to see Marge on TV and remembered how much he had always liked her. When Marge, now squirming, tried to cut the evening short, Mike began to blubber about how lonely he was.

The audience cackled.

Leonard felt strangely weightless, as if the spring in his seat might lift him out altogether. On one hand, Mike Yanagita was a part, and better a part than no part at all. Steve Park had nailed it, his accent pitch-perfect, and he had more than held his own with Frances McDormand. And if people were laughing, it was only because they were *supposed* to laugh; it was a brilliant comic cameo in a movie where everyone was sent up. But when Emily slipped her hand into his and squeezed, he knew he wasn't crazy. The character was all the more sad and pathetic for being Asian. He didn't know how she knew; he was just grateful he didn't have to explain.

Then came the kicker: Marge learns from a friend that Mike hadn't really been married, that Linda Cooksey hadn't died of leukemia, that Mike had in fact been stalking Linda for a good year, that he had psychiatric problems and was now living with his parents. The thing was, Leonard liked the movie! He just wanted to like it without a caveat. As they walked out into the night, he knew as he'd always known but never in such a bone-deep way that the life he'd chosen was going to be hard, and that he'd never get through without someone like Emily.

———

When they reached the dunes, they sprang from the car, whooping like children, beckoned by hills of sand that rolled all the way down to water. They burned up a beach trail trimmed by dune grass, then pitched over the first brink, stumbling, buckling, sliding, down, down, down, both of them laughing.

Their first two years in L.A. had not been particularly kind. A few small roles here and there, but nothing to be proud of. They had moved in together, to save on rent as much as anything else. Then a mouthwash commercial that Leonard had done went national, and he made some major bank, and life seemed to catch air, take off. To celebrate, he flew them to the Oregon Shakespeare Festival in Ashland, where they stayed at a pretty Victorian inn and went to every single production, Shakespearean and otherwise, indoors and out. The weather was perfect, cool but not cold in the evenings, and they stayed up late over dinner, then nightcaps, sometimes in the hot tub at the inn, before sleeping in every morning. They had never had a better time.

After a week, they rented a car and drove two hours north to Crater Lake, Emily in cutoffs and aviators, feet on the dash, hands gypsying to music—Joni Mitchell, the Allman Brothers. When they reached the dazzling cobalt blue of the lake, they snapped pictures of themselves with a camera held at arm's length. Now, after three more hours of driving, they lay at the bottom of a dune corrugated by wind and gilded by sunset. Emily's hair was now chin-length. At the best of times, a few strands were always escaping the feeble tuck of her ears. Out here, in the wind, it blew about wildly. When she nestled her face on his chest, it seemed the great mystery of his life—of any life—had been solved. The feeling had seized him before but never as surely as now.

"Let's get married!" he shouted over the breaking waves.

She threw back her head and laughed. "Yes, yes, yes, yes!"

———

Three evenings a week, they went to the gym. That was just part of the deal in L.A., the regimen of being an actor, going on four years now. But one night, getting ready, Emily flopped on the couch and said, "I'm too tired to go."

"Up and at 'em," Leonard said, wagging her foot.

Her foot jerked. "Len, I'm *exhausted.*"

They'd both had long days, traversing the city as usual, but he feared her exhaustion ran deeper. In the past six months, besides some work as an extra, she'd been cast only in a fringy play and a one-line role in a daytime soap. Worse, she'd made it through the preread and the callback and the studio test for a TV pilot until she found herself in a screening room with a dozen network executives, her test deal already signed, and she killed it, absolutely killed it, but still didn't get the part. She should have been encouraged. Instead, she mourned what had seemed like her last best chance. It terrified him, the thought of her giving up.

"Come on," he said, "we have to."

She sat up abruptly and stared at him. Then she marched to the bedroom, changed into workout gear, and left with him in silence. Of course, now that he'd gotten his way, he felt like an asshole. And of course, that would be the night she wound up dropping a dumbbell on her foot. They were at one of those densely packed warehouse-sized gyms, going through their routine in steely silence when a plated dumbbell she was hoisting from the rack slipped through her fingers. She cried out but wouldn't stop, kept lifting, eyes damp. As soon as they got home, she took Tylenol and went to bed.

The next day, she came home as he was making dinner. Right away, he could tell that her limp had gotten worse. That morning her foot had looked okay, but now, as she toed off her flats with a wince, her foot looked gruesomely livid and swollen.

"You should see a doctor."

"We can't afford it."

"Just put it on a credit card."

"No way."

Even if she wasn't accusing him, he felt guilty. He really didn't know where all the money had gone. Outside of the trip to Oregon and a small wedding at a ranch in the Santa Monica Mountains, he had hardly splurged on anything. True, he had stopped waiting tables for a while, but that was a calculated gamble, one she had supported. He had also done responsible things like buy them health insurance, but precisely because he'd spent the money then, he no longer had it now.

She toughed it out for a few more days, but when she started to weep with every step, he drove her to Good Samaritan. Eventually they were seen by a foot surgeon, a bronzed, white-haired man in scrubs who said something to someone about going to Fiji as he entered the room. He took one look at the X-rays and recommended surgery.

"What's it going to cost?" Emily asked.

"Four, maybe five thousand dollars."

Emily flicked her eyes at Leonard. "What's the worst that can happen if I don't have surgery?"

"Might not heal properly."

"Can I have surgery later, if it doesn't?"

The surgeon shrugged. "Maybe. It depends."

Emily stood. "Then I'll take my chances."

Leonard desperately wanted to say no—and hated that he couldn't.

"What line of work are you in?" the surgeon asked.

When Emily wouldn't answer, Leonard said, "My wife's an actor."

"I figured. You have the look," the man said, which seemed ironic. Pretty as she was, she was never quite *something* enough for Hollywood. "They only care about my weight," she often complained. "My weight and my cup size." Leonard was built and clean-cut, but no one ever took *him* for an actor.

"If I were an actor," the surgeon continued, "I wouldn't want crooked toes."

"No one's looking at my feet."

"You'd be surprised," the man replied. Then, sighing: "At least get yourself a boot. It should only run you fifty bucks."

After the medical store, Emily lay on their mustard-colored couch as Leonard iced her foot. Like just about everything else, the couch had come from a thrift store. Emily had a talent for thrift, for conjuring style from mismatched cutlery and dinnerware. He had often been struck by how lived-in her apartment was—in his, the mattress had always lain on the floor—which was why when the time came he had moved in with her.

"It's been four years, Len."

"I know."

"I just don't know if I have what it takes."

"Hey, hey," he said, sitting down in the crook of her waist and tucking in a few strands of her hair.

"I'm already twenty-seven."

"You're *only* twenty-seven. In the grand scheme of

things, four years is nothing. Think of the people we know who got their breaks later. That's the great thing about being an actor. It's not like being an athlete. We can do this till we're ninety."

"Oh, god," she said, covering her damp eyes and laughing. "I already feel . . . old and stale. How many auditions have I done? How many pilot seasons? I see the same CDs, the same directors, the same producers—and they've all seen me. I'm not a fresh face anymore."

After four years, L.A. had gotten into their blood, but they had started to flirt with the thought of leaving. They couldn't help feeling above the studio system, even as they tried to claw their way into it. Every compromise, all the hamming instead of acting, it was starting to get to them. Plus, they missed the briskness of fall, the first snap of winter.

He said, "Let's move to New York."

She looked at him.

"Yeah, let's move to New York!" he said, suddenly taken. "Think about it. No one will know us. We can start over. A clean slate. Besides, we're made for the stage, not this studio bullshit—not that we won't keep trying." Part of him wasn't ready to leave. Grinding as L.A. was, he still had faith. But he was afraid that if he pushed too hard something other than bone might break.

He clutched her shoulders. "What do you say?"

Her eyes filled. Then she wiped her cheeks with the heels of her hands, and he couldn't decipher her feelings, whether she was angry at him for not letting her quit or sad at the thought of leaving L.A.—the dreams they had chased and the life they had made—or happy to be leaving at last, getting out, starting over.

Or all of the above.

———

Their first place in the city was a shotgun apartment on the Lower East Side, in the crotch between the Manhattan and Williamsburg bridges. The front door opened onto the living room, which led in turn to the bedroom with two streetside windows, the only sources of light in the whole place. On the other side of the living room was a one-wall kitchen and a step-up bathroom, its door only two feet wide. They had gotten rid of most of their things, left it to friends or the curb in L.A., none of it worth much of anything. They had sold their cars, too, and driven a rental cross-country, without stopping, eager to save money, to get on with life, the two of them taking turns, sleeping while the other drove, so maniacal about it that the woman at the rental agency in New York had arched a brow, wondering how they had managed to defy space-time.

That first day, lured by the sound of salsa, they found their way to El Sombrero, the place they would visit again and again for black bean soup and sopapillas. Then they stumbled across Orchard Street. It was a Sunday, the road closed to traffic, and tables and racks full of discount bras and bags and hats and shoes filled the street, the smell of new leather so heady that Emily thought she was back on the festival circuit. They didn't know that the Lower East Side was on the cusp of becoming something else. In less than three years, they would have to move, chased away by hipsters and high rent. But that first day, poking through Judaica stores, buying pickles from sidewalk barrels, they felt themselves following the migrants of old: Germans, Italians, Irish, Jewish, Chinese. That night, after christening the apartment on an air mattress, they ventured out to Chinatown for a bowl of noodles at midnight. They had reached the beacon, the mecca, and they couldn't get enough.

———

The morning after the third performance of *Lear*, Leonard rode the 1 train down to 34th Street, then entered the bowels of Penn Station. Through the scissoring crowd, he spotted Derek, who also had a duffel bag over his shoulder. In the company's second season, Derek had played Puck in *A Midsummer Night's Dream*. They'd been friends ever since.

"Season opener, dude," Derek said, holding out a fist.

This was their first school presentation of the year, and one of the ways that Leonard made a go of things. It wasn't easy, just a couple hundred bucks here and there, but summer had been fallow and Emily was gone. Every little bit helped.

Today they were going to P.S. 82 in Queens. On the Long Island Rail Road, Leonard said, "Haven't seen you at the show."

"Yeah, sorry, dude. Had some things this weekend with the Legion."

Derek was a member of the Empire City Garrison of the 501st Legion, a volunteer group that showed up at events in screen-ready *Star Wars* costumes. As far as Leonard could tell, Derek was running off to these things every weekend.

"Doesn't Min-ji want you to spend time with the kids? I mean, don't *you* want to?"

"As long as I bring home the bacon, bro."

Eight years ago, Derek had been one of the actors Leonard saw again and again at the same auditions, but as soon as he was done with *A Midsummer Night's Dream*, he went and got an MBA. Now he worked on Wall Street. His economic forecasts were always gloomy—the country was awash in too much credit and going the way of Japan—but he himself was doing just fine. For instance, he owned not one but *two* *Star Wars* costumes, Darth Vader and Boba Fett, each at a cost of thousands of dollars. His pride and joy was Boba Fett's helmet, made in Italy and weathered with total screen accuracy.

After getting off at Jamaica Station, they passed pizza parlors, hair salons, and 99¢ stores until they reached a side street, half-lined with houses. Something he and Emily had never agreed on was whether or not to buy a house. Emily had wanted a house, any house, as long as it was theirs. But what would they have been able to afford except maybe something out here? One of these weird little houses with metal awnings that looked out onto the backs of warehouses.

P.S. 82 was a red-brick building with stark white

cornerstones. They were greeted by two outstretched trees and a rubber welcome mat with a pixelated rainbow of children. After checking in with an armed security guard, they followed the principal, Ms. Hernandez, to the teachers' lounge, where they changed into stockings, breeches, and doublets.

When Leonard had first started doing these shows, it hadn't taken long to figure out that the Bard didn't hold much sway with children. Only two things did, comedy and swordplay, so that's what they stuck to. They appeared onstage from opposite wings, Leonard as Hal and Derek as Hotspur. When Hotspur said, "I can no longer brook thy vanities," they drew. What followed was a long, lusty routine, all the more dramatic for their shields, which clanged like garbage cans. A sea of sweet brown faces cheered, then roared when Hotspur was killed.

"That was a scene from *The History of Henry IV* by William Shakespeare," Leonard said, panting, "who was born in England in . . ."

Next they did the balcony scene from *Romeo and Juliet*. Derek stood atop a ladder in a long, flowing wig, cooing in a high-pitched voice, and the children knew enough to laugh.

In the final part of the show, they played Mercutio and Tybalt, this time with two rapiers apiece. They had done the show so many times that they hadn't bothered rehearsing, not even after the long layoff, and Leonard was pleased by how easily it all came back to him, until Derek swiped his rapier at Leonard's head, and Leonard forgot to duck. Luckily, he flinched, and the rapier struck his shoulder before glancing off his head. Nonetheless, a tuning fork sounded inside his skull, and he stumbled. From his knees, he touched his throbbing scalp and came away with blood. Derek stepped forward, as if to help, then caught himself.

"I am hurt. A plague o' both your houses!" Leonard managed before carrying through to the end.

"Shit, dude, you all right?" Derek asked offstage.

"Yeah, I'm fine. Sorry, my bad."

After posing for pictures and signing a few autographs, they collected their checks from the principal, who seemed unaware that anything had gone awry, despite the blood crusting in Leonard's hair. On the train back, Derek reached into his wallet and pulled out two hundred-dollar bills.

"Check's in my name, so here's cash."

"What for?"

"You're gonna need stitches."

Derek, of course, didn't need the money. He just took every chance he got to put on a costume.

"Nah, man, that's cool," Leonard said. "I've got Obamacare now."

"Here, take it," Derek insisted, his voice surprisingly shaky. "Me and Min-ji have been meaning to have you over . . ."

Only it was too sad, too awkward. That's what he meant. Leonard was now leprously unattached, and he could hear Min-ji say, *No, don't, it'll be weird.*

Leonard waved the money away. "Spend it on the kids."

———

On a downy winter night in New York, as the two of them lay in a swaddle of covers, Emily placed a hand on his chest. "Let's have a baby."

Leonard had always imagined children in his life, and whenever they talked of children—distantly, hypothetically—they talked of more than one, but her sudden expectancy filled him with dread.

"Now?"

The temperature dropped a tick. "Soon, don't you think? I'm almost thirty."

After two years in New York, Leonard could feel midlife encroaching, time no longer quite on their side. The last thing he wanted to be was one of those fathers who was too old to keep up. Worse, almost as soon as they had moved, his mother had started showing signs of trouble, forgetting words, names, even where she was. Stranger still, she went from a lifetime of painting traditional Chinese landscapes to an obsession with abstract colors and shapes, as if possessed by Kandinsky. His father pressed for a grandchild, and Leonard felt a certain need to oblige. But he was almost thirty-five. Almost thirty-five and still trying to make it. A baby would land in his life with all the subtlety of a hand grenade. If anything, he needed to double down, spend *more* time trying, not less. The irony was, his father might have gotten a grandchild sooner if not for his own countervailing pressure. "People always ask how you're doing. What am I supposed to tell them?" Leonard raged for a better answer.

"I thought we agreed," he said to Emily. "Not until we have health insurance."

Every Thursday, they picked up a copy of *Backstage* at the nearest newsstand and combed through the casting calls, but they weren't yet members of SAG or AFTRA or Actors' Equity. The problem was, you couldn't get a union job without being a union member, but you couldn't be a union member without having had a union job. A genuine Catch-22, and he and Emily had yet to be let into the club. The only other way was to earn enough points, but they hadn't managed that, either. Many mornings, they got down to Actors' Equity on 46th Street by 5:00 a.m. for the non-union postings, then waited all day for auditions, sometimes auditioning for roles that had already been cast. Most of the hopefuls, red-eyed and caffeinated, were women, a cavalcade of starlets, but even so, Leonard and Emily couldn't decide who had it harder between them.

"Who knows when we'll get insurance at this rate," Emily said, her hand still on his chest. "It might be another year or two, even if we do summer stock. I was thinking . . . maybe we could ask your parents for help."

When he didn't reply, she said, "I'd ask my mom but you know her, she lives hand-to-mouth. I think your parents really want a baby. Your dad is always pulling me aside—"

"I can't ask my dad."

"Why not?"

When he'd skipped seeing his parents on the way back from London, he thought it would only be a matter of time before he went home triumphant. But that was years ago now.

"You know why, Emily."

"But your mom's getting worse."

The thought lashed him, especially since he should have been doing more to help his father, who found his wife's condition shameful. "Crazy catatonic disease" it was called in Chinese.

"He might have to put her in a home. It's not a good time to ask. We can do this ourselves. We just have to be patient."

She looked at him as if to place him, her eyes little convex mirrors, shrinking the room in duplicate. Then she pulled her hand away and gazed at the ceiling, leaving a cooling spot on his chest. A few months ago, they had lain in the dark much like this as the city sent a comet tail of smoke and ash into the universe, not two miles from their apartment, only then they had held on tightly, taken refuge in each other.

He took her hand and laid it back on his chest.

"We've got time. We'll have kids, I promise."

———

A year and half later, he found himself in the back of a cab, Emily slumped against him in a flaming red dress, her face in the crook of his neck. At the gala, they'd had too much to drink, and now she was lying across the seat—shoes off, legs tucked under. The city slid past, kaleidoscopic.

The year before, Emily had played Honey in an off-Broadway revival of *Who's Afraid of Virginia Woolf?* She wasn't as pinched and neurotic-looking as Sandy Dennis in the movie, but she had a power all her own, and Leonard wasn't surprised when the Lortel Awards came calling. At last the world was taking note of what he'd always known.

A few weeks before the ceremony, they went to Bergdorf Goodman on Fifth Avenue to shop for a dress. Each one she tried on seemed more beautiful and obscenely expensive than the last. "Let's go. This is crazy," Emily said under her breath. He didn't want to say, *This might be as close as you'll ever get.* He believed she had more Lortels and Obies and Tonys in her yet. But he knew life was fickle, so when she tried on a backless red gown that only came out to a month's rent, he convinced her to buy it.

The ceremony took place at the Lucille Lortel Theatre in the West Village. The show featured five musical numbers, including one with puppets and a tribute to Stephen Sondheim. Emily didn't win, but it didn't matter. At the gala afterward, she looked positively radiant as people—stars!—came up to shake her hand or kiss her on the cheek. Watching, Leonard felt proud, relieved, and yes, jealous. Not so much of her, though he felt that, too, but of the men who now lavished attention and made her laugh, her mouth a bright ring the color of her dress. They made him feel dispensable, like a booster rocket falling away, and he had the aching feeling she was going to leave him. Maybe that's why he'd kept hitting the open bar all night.

Now he was riding in the back of a cab, watching the city go by and feeling strangely unmoored.

"Happy?" he said.

She purred.

"I'm proud of you."

She nuzzled closer, breath lush. "It's all so ironic, don't you think?"

"What is?"

"Me playing Honey."

"Why?"

"That's who I played the first time we met!"

"Are you drunk?"

"Yes. What's your point?"

"That wasn't Albee."

She sat up. "What are you talking about?"

He shrugged. "It wasn't Albee."

"Of course it was."

"No, it wasn't."

"Then who was it?"

To his dismay, he couldn't remember the name of the play or the playwright. "It was contemporary. You know, the one about infidelity."

"Well, that narrows it down."

"Look, I remember very clearly."

"*I* remember very clearly."

They went around and around. They *had* played Nick and Honey, he said, but that was later, after they started dating. Emily, buzzed, accused him of confusing *wanting* to sleep with her with having already done so. This wasn't the argument he wanted to have on this of all nights, so he gave in. Maybe he was wrong, he was drunk, too. Either way, he was surprised—and pained—that they couldn't agree on the past.

———

After a couple of hours at the ER, Leonard stood in front of his bathroom mirror, holding back his hair to see the sutures. Four neat stitches, like a mini football. The nurse had been swift and distractingly chatty, but he'd still felt that curved needle tugging like a fish hook.

When he couldn't crane his neck any longer, he leaned against the sink and studied his face, as actors are wont to do. He looked pretty good for his age, but his age was starting to show. These days, every little flaw set off tiny peals of alarm. Not everyone could have a face like Om Puri, ravaged with character. Worse, he now faced the specter of a much deeper flaw. He hoped it was only rust, but there was no telling.

To kill time before the show, he decided to watch a movie. This was usually the time of year he was showing movies to some young actor crashing on the couch who didn't seem to know there was Asian American cinema before *Harold & Kumar*. He often began with *The Cheat* starring Sessue Hayakawa, who played what might have been the original sexual menace. But at least DeMille had cast an Asian in an Asian role, unlike Griffith a few years later—and any number of directors since. And apparently women had *swooned* for Hayakawa, this a hundred years ago, as if time were moving backward.

Today he settled on *Hud*. James Wong Howe was the cinematographer—and won an Oscar!—so it counted. As soon as his laptop roused with a sentient whir, he thought of calling Emily. Sometimes they still texted, mostly old married-couple stuff, as if they were shouting from different rooms. Had she thrown out his old sneakers? Did she know where the iPod shuffle was? The few times they had talked on the phone they had lapsed into oceanic silence, each waiting, it seemed, for the other to cave.

Before he could dial, though, a marimba sounded. Mackenzie, his agent, the latest in a string of them. This one was blond, prep-schooled, and half his age, an intern-turned-assistant now building her own list. "Middle-aged divorcé on the prowl," she said, describing the part. "That's you. No offense. But the audition has to be, like, tomorrow?" Suddenly he realized why he was holding out on Emily: a big break could still change the rules of engagement. He knew better, but as soon as he got off the phone, he felt a flicker of hope, that old nemesis.

———

Six years after moving to New York, during what might have been his nadir, Leonard went to see his agent, Richard Luntz. Richard had given him the pilot for a new Showtime series, and Leonard wanted to talk. Richard's office was tucked away in a squat building in Hell's Kitchen. Like so many others in the city, the building had once been something else, in this case a bank, the shame of its obsolescence still etched in stone.

They shook hands across a desk citied with papers, Richard languorously, without rising. Clearly he thought that Leonard had come to lavish him with praise. The two of them had met at a party where a bearded and balding Richard had gone around handing out business cards. Leonard had found the card chintzy-looking but knew for that reason that they were the same-sized fish.

"Listen, I appreciate you setting up this audition—"

"You better. It was a bitch, let me tell you."

"Here's the thing—"

"You know who's going to play the lead?" Richard asked. "That guy from *Six Feet Under*."

"Which guy?"

"You know, the gay brother. What's his name."

"I love that show," Leonard mumbled, almost to himself.

"That's what I'm talking about! Red carpets, Emmy awards. This is big time!"

For a moment Leonard indulged the fantasy: the limo, the tux, the jockeying microphones, Emily beside him in haute couture. More fantastical still, the steady work, the dignity. It was almost enough to make him shut his big fat mouth. But unlike the lead in this new series, who apparently had no conscience, Leonard did, and it rankled. His character was "slight, half Japanese, half white." That he was none of these things was the least of his worries.

"Here's the thing, though. I'm not sure I want this role."

Richard brayed. "Good one, funnyman."

"I'm serious."

Light drained from Richard's face. "What the hell are you talking about?"

"I don't mind that he's a geek," Leonard said. "A forensic investigator actually sounds kind of cool. But he's also a freak and a perv."

"Oh, Christ."

"No, listen," Leonard said, retrieving the script from his messenger bag and thumbing through the marked pages. "The first time we meet the character, Masuka, we're told that something's wrong with him. He has a fake smile, as if he learned how to smile from models in a Sears catalog, and he has a laugh that sounds like he's drowning, to the point where the main character wonders if he should perform CPR or the Heimlich maneuver." Leonard slapped the script with the back of his hand. "Come on, dude's a freak."

"For fuck's sake, Leonard."

"Wait, I'm not done. The first time Masuka meets the main character's sister, he offers her a hundred bucks to put his head between her 'babaloos.' She offers to stomp on his dick, and he starts laughing in that crazy way of his, and she stares at him with disgust. You want me to be excited about this?"

"You're missing the point," Richard said, leaning forward,

fingers spread beseechingly. "This is a show about a serial killer. *Everyone* is a freak."

That was the other thing, the very premise of the show. Some people got to be every kind of crazy when he just wanted to be normal. To see himself in a story.

"A good serial killer? Is that even possible?"

Richard's eyes flared. "Who do I look like? Sigmund Freud?"

Leonard laughed. If Richard's beard were white and he wore a pair of round glasses . . . But laughing only set Richard off.

"You know what your problem is, Leonard? You're a prude. Anyone who makes it anywhere in this industry has to bend over and take it, but you're too much of a goddamn prude."

When Leonard had pointed out the same problems in the script to Emily, she hadn't said much, just shook her head—at the script, yes, but at him, too, or so it seemed. For her sake, he was almost willing to bite the bullet. But he was tired of playing grocers and gangsters, of having yet another snot-nosed MFA student tell him to thicken up the accent. All he wanted was a role he didn't have to explain.

"Look," Richard said, soft-pedaling, "just get the part and go down to Miami. That's where they're filming. Did I mention that? Go down and enjoy the sun and get away"—he gestured at the dome of cloud outside—"from all this."

Leonard was desperate. Absolutely desperate for something to happen. Yet somehow he convinced himself that years from now, when he was famous and telling this story, maybe at the Actors Studio, his current desperation would only underscore the courage of his stance.

He dropped the script on Richard's desk, to a plosion of dust. "Sorry, I can't."

"If you don't go to this fucking audition," Richard said, pointing, "I'm dropping you, Xiao."

When Leonard tuned in for the pilot, he realized right away that the script played better onscreen. The role of Masuka had gone to a short Korean American actor Leonard knew in passing. The character was still a little suspect, but they'd cut the lines about the Sears catalog, about babaloos and stomping on his dick. Though it made him a little nauseated each time, Leonard forced himself to watch. But when the show got picked up for another season, then another and another, and the Emmys did in fact start rolling in, he and Emily had to stop.

———

Sometime after parting ways with Richard, when he realized he couldn't wait around for the world to see him as he saw himself, Leonard dreamed up the Asian American Shakespeare Company. He was fretting over his life, wondering what to do, when he thought of the day John Barton, the guru himself, had come to Central's tiny campus in Hampstead. Leonard had been on the contemporary acting track, which began with Early Modern, and

when he took a turn as Claudio from *Measure for Measure*—
"The weariest and most loathèd worldly life / That age,
ache, penury, and imprisonment / Can lay on nature is
a paradise / To what we fear of death"—the great man
had said, "Good. Well relished," which made Leonard feel
anointed. It had been such a beautiful time in his life, London. Back then, all was potential, and that feeling charged
his memories of the Oregon Shakespeare Festival and the
L.A. Women's Shakespeare Company and the African-
American Shakespeare Company in San Francisco, which
he and Emily had driven up one year to see, and all these
particles that had long bumped around in his mind finally
coalesced.

He carried around the idea for a while without saying
anything to Emily. After her cool response to his complaints
about the Showtime series, he was afraid she wouldn't understand. Sure enough, when he finally brought it up, she
seemed a little bewildered.

"A theater company?" she asked.

By this point they had moved from the Lower East Side
to Morningside Heights, into the churn of students around
Columbia and Barnard, and they were sitting in bed with
the window open, serenaded by the ambience of Amster-
dam Avenue. Her Lortel nomination had put off talk of
kids, but that was a couple of years ago now. It bothered
him, the way she was trying to figure out how his plans
might impede her own. Easy to abjure success when you've
already had it. It felt like they'd been waiting in a long line

for a party, but now that she was in, chatting away, drink in hand, she forgot he was still standing out in the cold.

"I can start small. With a showcase. If the show does well, it could get picked up for a longer run. Or someone might see me. If nothing else, I need a new agent." When this sounded self-serving, he said, "It'll be a good platform for everyone. Maybe we can launch a *few* careers."

"Won't a showcase be expensive?"

By the law of Actors' Equity, a showcase couldn't cost more than $20,000. A pittance by Broadway standards but still way more than they could afford.

"Don't worry, I'll find the money."

"What play are you thinking?"

"*Hamlet.*" As soon as he said it aloud, he heard the ostentation. "You know, before I get too old."

He waited for her to assure him. Instead, she just nodded. That girl who had taken his hand during *Fargo*—where had she gone?

———

A few weeks later, reading in bed, Leonard turned to Emily and said, "Do you know there's another version of Hamlet's soliloquy?"

"Really?"

"Yeah, the First Quarto is totally different."

Emily closed her book and leaned over his shoulder. "Let me see."

"I've got a better idea." He climbed out of bed with book in hand. His boxers didn't lend themselves to the moment, but he felt he had something to prove.

> *To be or not to be—aye, there's the point,*
> *To Die, to sleep, is that all? Aye, all:*
> *No, to sleep, to dream, aye, marry, there it goes,*
> *For in that dream of death, when we awake,*
> *And borne before an everlasting Judge,*
> *From whence no passenger ever returned,*
> *The undiscovered country, at whose sight*
> *The happy smile, and the accursed damned . . .*

"I like it," she said when he finished the whole speech. "It's lively. It plays well."

"That's it!" he said, snapping and pointing theatrically. "I'll stage the First Quarto. I mean, this whole thing is already kind of . . . renegade. Why not do—"

"An unexpected version."

"An *unauthorized* version."

Her brows furrowed. "What do you mean?"

"The First Quarto isn't really Shakespeare."

"How can anyone say for sure? What is or isn't? It was so long ago."

"No, the First Quarto was put together by actors from memory. And you can't trust memory."

———

In the early years, the company ran on a shoestring and adrenaline. That first year, they rented a dingy black box theater, but it still cost two thousand a week, so they had to pull everything off in just seven days. To save $75 a night on a fire marshal, Emily, to her credit, hopped two trains and a bus to Brooklyn to take the fire safety test herself. Leonard, for his part, called in every favor with actors he knew, none of whom got paid.

The day the one-column review came out in the *Times*, he ran home to read it with Emily. The show was described as "agile" but "uneven"—"Fair enough," Leonard said— but he was praised for a "credible" performance. "Listen to this," he said. "'The *Hamlet* that generations have come to know and love in fact reads better on the page. Staging the more theatrical First Quarto was an inspired choice.'"

"That can be the blurb on the next poster," Emily said, blocking words in the air. "'Inspired'—*The New York Times!*"

———

Despite the stitches, the Thursday night show went off brilliantly. The next day, Leonard felt good as he took the 1 train down to Tribeca, emerging at the five points of Chambers, Hudson, and West Broadway. He was dressed in khakis and a loud Hawaiian shirt, *a middle-aged divorcé on the prowl*, his résumé and headshot lying snugly in the pocket of his messenger bag. He hadn't been given sides, but he still had to get in the zone, which was how he almost missed Emily, walking down the other side of Broadway.

She looked striking, the way people do after an absence, as if they've gone out of their way to improve. Her hair was longer, flipped at the ends, and her face looked made up, more deeply etched, as if a drawing done in pencil had finally been inked. What hadn't changed was her talent for simple outfits, in this case a white blouse and a pair of knee-high boots that made her slim-fitting jeans look like jodhpurs. Even from across the street, her green eyes luminesced. For months now, he'd been hoping for just such an encounter, but now that it was here, he felt flat-footed.

He was just about to call out when he realized she wasn't alone. Without thinking, he ducked behind a car and peered over the roof. The man she was with was tall and dark-skinned, and she gazed at him attentively. In response to something he said, she stopped and put a hand to her mouth, stooping with laughter. Then she slipped a hand into his. Leonard had been keeping tabs on social media, fearing precisely this, but nothing had prepared him. His breath grew short and his heart so engorged he could feel its shape, its weirdly elliptical sloshing. The guy looked mon-eyed, like some Wall Street dude bro. Was that what she was into now? At one point, she drew closer, touching her head to his shoulder. Somehow, in that moment, he knew she wasn't done, she was going to try again—for a child.

As soon as they were out of sight, he sat down on the pavement. *I had been happy if the general camp, / Pioneers and all, had tasted her sweet body, / So I had nothing known.* Now he knew what those words meant.

He wanted to go home. No longer gave a flying fuck. No longer understood, in fact, why he had ever chased the dream. Yet he went through with the audition, out of sheer force of habit. Looked into the camera and slated like a zombie. By dumb luck, he was given a scene in which the middle-aged divorcé mourns the passing of his old life, so he read without embellishment, chin pitted and trembling. "Wow, okay," the casting assistant said, unreadably. Outside, Leonard straight-armed the nearest wall and pinched the corners of his eyes, undone at last.

———

After her star turn as Honey, Emily was riding high and tried to parlay that role into bigger and better things. In the two years that followed, she landed a couple more off-Broadway shows and a few fleeting credits on television, but she never quite caught the wave, never reached the same heights. Instead, her star faded, to the point where Leonard wondered if she wasn't letting go, happy with what she'd accomplished and eager to move on. So he wasn't surprised the night she said, "I think it's time to have a baby."

Four years ago, on that wintry night on the Lower East Side, the thought of a baby had filled him with dread, but now the feeling was gone. She was right, it was time. She had given him the things he'd needed, including *Hamlet*, but they couldn't wait on him forever. It was too late for his mother, who could no longer recognize him, much less some strange new being, but there was still his father, and Emily above all. He sensed her need to remake her childhood, to rectify the past, all those nights of sleeping in her mother's car, and he'd kept her waiting long enough. Kept them both. He was ready. Ready as he'd ever be.

That night, they made love sweetly, just at the prospect. A few months later, when her body was ready, her systems flushed, they started trying in earnest. As soon as it seemed plausible, they picked up a test at the nearest Duane Reade. They were surprised but not discouraged by the single blue line. They knew lots of people who had tried for longer, then boom, magic.

But the scene would repeat itself, month after month after month. At first there had been some joy, some hopeful affection, but trying came to seem more and more like work, especially when they started using a monitor. First thing every morning, Emily would check its despotic little screen to see if she had to do a urine test. If she did, she would march to the bathroom with a little stick. If it was a "peak" or even "high" day, she would arrange herself on pillows, summoning every force in the universe. Sometimes she looked a little irritated, as if she resented his having a part, and it seemed unfair to them both, how they had to wait for everything.

———

They had to try for a year before they qualified for anything through insurance. Then they were given permission to take a battery of tests. More than once, Emily lay stirruped, her lower body covered in something like a modesty sheet, which only seemed more immodest. Leonard, for his part, had to suffer a long, probing needle. Insurance, however, didn't cover the acronyms: IVF, ICSI, GIFT, ZIFT. The best they could do was take Clomid and Letrozole and eat better and exercise more, drink less coffee and booze, and, in his case, floss more and keep his balls cooler—no more laptops on the lap—and watch porn, which supposedly helped his count . . .

Then, in the middle of everything, Leonard lost his insurance, hadn't worked enough in the past six months to keep it, and Emily verged on the same. They still waited tables as they almost always had, Leonard for years in a white shirt and skinny black tie at a brasserie in Soho. ("Are you Vietnamese?" he was sometimes asked because the place was French.) But work, *real* work, had dried up for both of them, all at once, even the sundry parts that usually kept them afloat and in good standing with the unions, maybe because they'd been distracted, focused on other things, and Emily needed to land a gig pretty much right away or time would run out and they'd have to stop trying, after almost two years of trying. And by now Emily had wearied, her eyes ever more sunken.

The night she got a call from her agent about a callback, neither of them could sleep. Gone were the days when a callback meant hopeful chatter, holding up outfits, running lines; now they just lay awake with their own thoughts. At one point Emily began to cry. It started confusingly, with silent shudders, as if she were laughing, then flourished into racking sobs, and it scared him. He wanted to hold her but feared the tensing flinch.

In the morning, after she left for the callback, he went out to Duane Reade, this time for a bottle of Robitussin, though neither was sick. Robitussin thinned mucus, including cervical mucus, and friends of theirs swore that it worked. After a burly dude with tunnel earrings gave him back his change, Leonard had just enough for a breakfast burrito next door if he wanted. Then he saw that the Mega Millions jackpot was a few days away and over $60 million. He hated being short on cash, always having to choose. Did he buy that slice of pizza and walk or did he take the subway and go hungry? In this case, though, the choice was easy. If Emily didn't get the part, they would need a Hail Mary.

He carried the ticket around for days, talismanically, sensing a kind of heat in his pocket. When he finally threw it away a week later, he buried it in the trash to make sure Emily wouldn't see it.

———

The leaves were starting to turn, the swelter gone from their apartment. Leonard had just come home with a bag of groceries—was still holding it, in fact—when Emily walked in, stricken.

"What's up?"

She stood awkwardly for a moment before sitting on the couch, slipping her purse from her shoulder in that practiced way of hers. "I have some things to tell you. But don't be mad."

His first thought: an affair. Short-lived, meaningless, over. It wasn't impossible to think. Sex had become a chore, and some magnanimous part of him hoped she had done it just for fun, even as he felt the gut punch. So it came as a relief when she said, "I didn't get the part." Then came the aftershock, the implications.

"Okay," he said. "Okay."

"And I went to the doctor's. I'm sorry. I'm sorry I didn't tell you, but I didn't want to put you through another—"

"*And?*"

A nod, a smile. Eyeshine.

He dropped the groceries, heard the wet pop of a jar as he lunged, and faintly rued what he'd done as he toppled her.

———

They entered a brave new world of folic acid, omega-3s, and sudden privations: no wine, no sushi, no Brie, and just one cup of coffee a day.

"Remember that place in L.A. we used to go to for *yukhoe?*" Emily asked. "After the baby is born, I'm going to eat a boatload of that."

He pictured the restaurant in Koreatown. "What was the name of that place?"

Emily caressed her brows. "Wow, I can't remember."

"We used to go there all the time."

"I know. I can see it. But I can't remember."

They'd had no choice but to ask his father for help. As soon as they did, Emily eased up on work. The odd short-term thing was fine, but there was no point in trying for roles she wouldn't be able to play in a month or two. Leonard, on the other hand, redoubled his efforts. He had six, maybe seven good months left. After that, who knew what would happen.

At twelve weeks, when she started to show, they found themselves in a darkened office, Emily lying on a padded table. After slathering a clear gel, the nurse pressed the scanner into Emily's belly with burrowing force. A wedge-shaped image leaped onscreen, like a flashlight cutting through darkness, and there it was, lying in its little hammock. Each time the nurse pressed down, emphatically, the baby would move, limbs flailing, like a floppy marionette. The nurse drew some lines onscreen, then tapped the keyboard. That's when they heard the baby's heart, roaring along at 157 beats per minute.

"Everyone says 'peanut' or 'sweet pea' or 'jelly bean,'" Emily said afterward over ice cream, which she now craved constantly, even though the weather had turned. "We need something different."

He remembered the way the baby had moved. "Brits say 'poppet'—like 'puppet'—for 'darling.'"

"Poppet," she said, blooming. "I love it."

———

Two weeks later, he found bloodstained briefs in the hamper. "Everything okay?" he asked. "Just some spotting," Emily replied. "The midwife says it's no big deal. I had some in the first trimester too, remember?" He did and felt better.

But a few days later, as they were making dinner, Emily slicing thick tomato steaks on their tiger-striped cutting board, she cried out abruptly and doubled over.

"Are you okay?" Leonard asked, bracing her.

"Something's wrong."

On the ride to Mount Sinai St. Luke's, wet snow smeared the windows floridly. Emily lay in the back, head in his lap, an arm draped over her face. At the entrance to the hospital, as an orderly brought out a wheelchair, the cabdriver screamed for more money, above and beyond what appeared on the meter, and Leonard felt he had no choice but to fish for more bills and knew he would always remember that they were held to ransom in their hour of desperation. When the nurse pressed the scanner into Emily's belly, everything looked the same, the baby still there, still flopping around. Then, all at once, the Doppler wasn't whooshing and the heart wasn't blinking . . .

They were left to their anguish, their terrible lowing. Then they were given the option of a D&C, but Emily wouldn't hear of it, didn't want the baby coming out like that, so they went home and waited for things to take their course. When she started to soak through the sheets, she ran a bath and asked to be alone. For half the night, he stood with his head against the door as she bellowed and growled from the other side. A few times, he heard the tub empty, then fill again. Eventually all went quiet. When he opened the door, the room smelled of copper and the water looked so dark that he thought she'd bled out. But no, she sat with hands cupped, just staring. He got down next to the tub and looked for himself. God, he had never been more terrified, or more in love. They held her and kissed her and wouldn't let go.

———

After stumbling home from Tribeca, Leonard drew the curtains and curled up in bed, indifferent to the world. It felt like penance, lying there in darkness, replaying the things he'd seen, but also a kind of indulgence, kneading the injured parts of himself just to feel the ache.

He thought about calling. Maybe nothing had happened yet, or maybe whatever had happened didn't mean much, at least not enough to keep her from taking him back. Then he caught himself and felt foolish and couldn't see the point. He was angry at himself for not calling sooner, for misjudging their valence—and angry at her, too. He could no longer picture the other man's face but could still see his tailored suit, his bougie air, and it galled him to think that that was what she wanted.

He lay there all afternoon. When he wasn't thrashing in

the shallows of sleep, he was scrolling through his phone, falling down the rabbit hole of his own timeline. Their last meal out, their last visit to Pennsylvania, their last game at Yankee Stadium, both of them aging in reverse. Three years ago, after his mother died, his father had driven her ashes on a kind of farewell tour, past their house in West Cambridge, the shops they used to frequent in Chinatown, and the nursing home where she'd spent her final years. Staring at his screen, he felt himself doing the same, taking leave of what had once been life.

———

He dreaded the thought of having to perform that night, in a matter of hours. Never had the company seemed so unimportant. In his gloom, he thought of Marta, a woman he'd cast the year they put on *Macbeth*. Marta was twenty-five and fresh out of grad school, and during the table read, she'd cleared her throat and said, "Sorry, is this all we're doing? *Putting on* Shakespeare?"

Everyone was sitting at tables arranged in a large square, Marta directly across from him, her small frame belying the force of her presence.

"As opposed to what?"

"*Critiquing* Shakespeare. *Subverting* him."

Leonard felt a cool trickle down his spine. "By putting on Shakespeare, we're claiming our full-fledged humanity. That's subversive."

Marta shook her head, agitated. "Not subversive enough. Ask August Wilson. And no, Shakespeare does not represent 'humanity.' He represents the dead white European male notion of what it means to be human."

Leonard looked around to see if anyone might intercede, but everyone waited, shrinking and spellbound.

"So love, joy, sadness, grief—you're just going to cede those things?"

Marta made a face. "I'm not ceding anything. I just refuse to accept a narrow definition of what's universal. Shakespeare isn't a mirror held up to nature. He's a mirror held up to Western ontology."

"Then maybe we're advancing the radical notion that we're Westerners, too."

"But that's not how we see the world."

Somehow, this more than anything made Leonard seethe. "Are you saying we see the world with an 'Asian mind'? Sounds like Orientalism to me."

Marta shot up, chair scraping stridently. "Don't you fucking call me an Orientalist."

All eyes were downcast. All except Leonard's.

He said, "'I am human, I think nothing human alien to me.' Terence, the Roman playwright. When you're the director, you can direct however you like."

For a long moment, Marta rolled her lips. Then she shouldered her bag and left. The truth was, she had prodded his deepest fear, that the Asian American Shakespeare Company was little more than a novelty act, and a placating one at that, but he put on a brave face. When the door she'd pushed through finally snapped shut, he turned to the swing and said, "You're Hecate. Take it away."

———

When the time came, it was all Leonard could do to drag himself to the theater. On the train ride down, he stared at his greasy reflection in the window opposite, feeling queasy, the way he felt on early morning flights. What he wouldn't have given to stay in his dark little hovel.

But a funny thing happened: he was very good that night. It was partly exhaustion, which pumped him full of adrenaline, and partly his flayed sense of love, which brought him closer to Lear, but mostly it was no longer caring, which stripped him of all self-consciousness.

He started well the next night, too, soaring on the same narcotic, but he came down as the night wore on. In the fourth act, when he closed his eyes, pretending to be unconscious, he almost nodded off. Eventually he stirred, eyes fluttering. "You do me wrong to take me out o' th' grave," he said, and went on in that vein, confused, amnesic, until at last he recognized Cordelia. As always, he thought of his mother and her flukey moments of clarity. Today, though, the memory seemed to trip him. Sophie was kneeling, glassy-eyed. When she realized what was happening, she started blinking, wetting her cheeks, but he couldn't make sense of it. He tried not to panic. The audience wouldn't catch on for a few more seconds at least. For all they knew, this was simply a long look of recognition. One trick was movement; action could jog the mind. He couldn't well pace around, though, so he did what he could: he reached out and took Sophie's head in his hands, and she followed suit, gripping his wrists. Still nothing. But now that her face was half-hidden, she risked mouthing the words.

He let go, sat back. "Be your tears wet? Yes, faith. I pray, weep not," he said, as if nothing had happened.

After the show, Sophie sprang upon him. "You owe me a drink."

He was feeling spooked again, and old, in need of cheering.

"All right. Where to?"

As soon as they stepped through the door, he spotted the person he'd been hoping to see, standing next to a tree and its little wrought-iron fence, as if posing for a picture. She wasn't staring at her phone, feigning nonchalance. Instead, she stood with her hands in her pockets, heels together, toes apart, unabashedly waiting. This was something he had always loved about her, how guileless she could be.

"Emily."

She didn't say anything, just smiled, slouching a bit, one foot crossing the other. She was wearing a pair of black pants and a patterned blouse so thin he could see her camisole underneath.

"You were here tonight?"

She nodded.

"I didn't see you."

"I was in the back."

"Not my best night."

She smiled, sweet yet knowing. "You were great. And you, too."

Only then did he remember Sophie standing beside him, her expression now sullen. After hasty introductions—*This is my wife*, he almost said—he watched as Emily held out her hand serenely. She had always had a certain poise, but it pained him how unruffled she seemed.

"How are you doing?"

"Good."

"We were about to go for a drink. Want to join us?"

Sophie's face scrunched, and only then did Emily shift her eyes appraisingly. Now that they'd roused her suspicions, he wanted to say, *It's not what you think!*

"No, you go ahead. I just wanted to say I loved the show."

She looked as lovely as ever. She had always been soft and bright-eyed, but when she was young she had had an innocence that could sometimes be cloying. Now all that innocence had burned away. He wanted to turn to Sophie and say, *Sorry, I need to take a rain check*, but it wasn't good form, and he didn't want to look pathetic. Above all, he was afraid that even without Sophie, Emily would say, *Actually, I can't.*

"Okay. Another time."

"Another time."

As Emily turned away, she gave him the slightest curl of her lips and the smallest pinch of her brows, a sly, disapproving look that said, *A little young, don't you think?* and he felt it, the old telepathy. It gave him a little lift, even as she walked off without looking back.

———

Six months earlier, Leonard had sat at the kitchen table on a Saturday afternoon comparing versions of *Lear* in *The Oxford Shakespeare* and *The Riverside Shakespeare*, the text of each so small that he'd finally had to buy a pair of reading glasses. The day was unseasonably warm and Emily had suggested a walk by the river. But Leonard had said he wanted to work and she had stayed in the bedroom since.

Eventually she emerged. "Can we talk?"

"Can it wait?" he asked without looking up. "I'm on to something."

"No, Len, it can't."

She was wearing a scoop-neck T and a thick pair of sweatpants, and her face looked raw, as if she'd been crying. He peeled off his glasses.

"What's the matter?"

"I'm tired, Len. Tired of all of this."

An old, familiar groove. The tangle in his chest unwound. "You always say that."

"I'm telling you, I can't do this anymore."

The week before, she'd had a network test for another TV pilot. Once again, she had killed it, but once again, she didn't get the part. If that pilot in L.A. had seemed her last best chance, he could only imagine what she felt now. He had never understood why things hadn't taken off for her, why she hadn't had a career like the middling actors she often stood in for. She had always had as much talent, could do anything they could do except get the flywheel to catch.

"You almost got the pilot. It's not too late—"

"It *is* too late! I'm forty-two, Len. Women don't launch careers at forty-two."

When Emily had landed the role of Honey, it seemed a matter of getting older, growing into the right roles. Now it seemed they were growing *out* of them, if they hadn't already. Subtly, by degrees, she had stopped going for young romantic leads and going instead for middle-aged housewives and mothers, and each year the number of roles dwindled. To fill the gaps, she did more work as a stand-in, more classes at the Y.

"What are you going to do?"

"Anything else."

Lear to read, grants to write—he didn't want to get into it. Things would blow over as they always had.

"Okay," he said, slipping his glasses back on. "Whatever you want."

"No, Len, you don't understand." She sat down, reached across the table, and took his hands. "It's time. For both of us."

Like a dog pricking its ears, he sensed a change in the air. This moment had been a long time coming, and part of him felt relieved, as if he'd been desperately waiting for someone to wave the flag so he could at last rise from the trenches.

Then he felt a spout of anger and his own effort to suppress
it. Through his glasses, she looked a blur. He had to look
over them, admonishingly.

"What are you saying?"

"I can't chase the dream anymore."

He freed his hands. "Let's just give it a little more time."

"That's what you always say. How much more time can
we give it? It's been *twenty years*. Don't look at me like that,
Len. You can't say I haven't tried. I've given it everything.
Given *up* everything. What else do you want from me?"

"What about the company?"

"Maybe it's time to hand it off," she said, treading lightly.
"You've got a board now. They can find someone else."

The Asian American Shakespeare Company. It sounded
impressive, but what was it really? A tiny little theater that
still put on just one show a year, and a small one at that.
Yes, it had helped a few actors, but it hadn't launched *him*
onto Broadway or television or the big screen, and it certainly didn't make any money, not beyond what he paid
the actors and needed to keep things afloat. Yet he still
believed in what he was doing. Two years ago, the L.A.
Women's Shakespeare Company had shuttered its doors
after twenty years, but the African-American Shakespeare
Company was now an institution. He knew which way he
wanted to go.

"It's getting somewhere. It can still be something."

"It *is* something."

"It can be more."

"It can be more without you."

An old suspicion resurfaced. "You've never liked the company, have you?"

Her whole face bruised. "How can you say that?"

"You've always had mixed feelings."

"How many times have I taken the fire safety test? How many times have we had people on that couch?"

"Okay, you did your part—"

"Yes, I did my part. God, I can't believe you."

They sat there brooding. Then she took a different tack: she came over, sat on his lap, and draped her arms around him. "You'll always be the founder. It'll always be your legacy. I know it's hard, Len. It's hard for me, too. But you made a go of things. You've been on the stage in London, L.A., New York. Not everyone can say that."

"I thought I was going to be . . . more."

"It was harder for you than most. We both know why. But listen to me," she said, clamping his face. "I don't care about any of that anymore. Look at us. We're still here. That's all that matters."

"But what am I going to *do*?"

She paused to make her answer seem less rehearsed. "If I had a master's degree, I'd teach."

She'd been quietly urging him to take on a course—at City College, maybe, or Brooklyn College—as a step toward teaching full-time. Actors they knew had made the leap, but as far as he could tell, academia trailed only acting in its futility.

"There are hundreds of college towns," she said. "And each one probably has a theater, if you really want to scratch the itch."

So she wanted out of the city, too. For her sake, he tried to imagine it. Someplace they could hike more often, like they used to, where she could start the garden she was always talking about. Someplace that smelled of stagnant creeks and wood smoke, to which students returned each fall, in high spirits, and where he could take his rest each summer, maybe in a hammock in his own backyard, all while his 401(k) fattened for slaughter. It made a pretty picture. But then he thought of his father, who still harangued him all these years later—"When are you going to be serious?"— and he thought of the city on summer nights, on winter nights, the verve of it all.

"I can't."

She looked at him, those pale green eyes of hers startlingly close. Then she slid off his lap, sat on the couch, and raked her hands through her hair.

"I love acting, too. It saved my life. But it's not the only thing I wanted."

He drew up, sensing danger. "We tried."

"Did we?"

After they lost the baby, they had managed to avoid recriminations. If they hadn't, they might have blown apart. But six years later their scars had toughened.

"We tried again."

"I mean before."

He sighed. "We talked about it. We agreed. We didn't have insurance—"

"I mean before that."

"What are you talking about?"

"I wanted children long before New York."

He snorted, incredulous.

"Yes, I did. I started talking about kids as soon as we got married."

"Yeah, okay, everybody talks about kids in a hypothetical way—"

"It wasn't hypothetical. I wanted a baby."

"You're telling me you wanted a baby when you were twenty-five and trying to launch an acting career," he said, hoping she would hear the plain absurdity.

"Yes."

At moments like this, when they couldn't agree on the past, he imagined the past traveling as light through outer space. If only there were a way to outrace that light and train a powerful telescope back toward Earth, then they might yet know what really happened.

"You'd think I'd remember," he said.

"You'd think *I'd* remember! I *do* remember. I was always trying to tell you, but you wouldn't listen. You were always thinking about your career."

"And?"

"And we waited too long!"

This was what he'd always suspected, always feared: that she blamed him. But he never knew how deeply.

"Is that what you were thinking when you were hob-nobbing with Salma Hayek and Ed Norton?"

Her eyes widened. "You think I wouldn't trade that night in a heartbeat?"

He said nothing at first, chastened. "What choice did we have? We didn't have insurance."

"You could have asked your dad."

"I did ask my dad."

"What about after? When we still needed help? When we still had a chance?"

"You know why I couldn't."

She closed her eyes, drew a breath, composed herself. "I love you, Len, but I'm through with show business. I can't live like this anymore. I'm getting out while I still can. The only question is whether you're coming with me."

"I just need a little more time."

"Len, we've been talking about this for *years*. I'm done, I'm finally done. I'm leaving. The only thing harder than not making it is watching you—"

They carried on into the night, without bothering to eat or even turn on the lights, the darkness a salve. At one point, he stood by the window and looked out toward the double decks of the George Washington Bridge, where traffic appeared as two streams of light, one red, one white. When they had driven across the country, they had taken a northern route, through Vegas, Denver, Chicago, and Cleveland, and reached the city at dawn. As soon as they were past all the nothing on the New Jersey Turnpike, he woke her up. Crossing the bridge, they hollered, slapping the dash, the ceiling, Fort Washington Park as green and untouched as the day it was made. That was sixteen years ago. You couldn't grind away for that long without wondering if you'd wasted your life. Staked it all on some folly of youth. Maybe Emily was right. Maybe it was time to call it. Time to admit he was no one special. Just some guy endowed with consciousness, like billions and billions of others. But when he thought of joining the red stream out of the city, he just couldn't fathom it. Not after all this time. Not when his day was still coming.

They stayed up late, came close to making peace. In the middle of the night, she reached for him, face wet. In the morning she was gone.

———

"So you studied acting in Chicago?"

His weird sense of obligation had taken him and Sophie two blocks east to Jimmy's Corner, the only respectable place to drink in Times Square, enshrined with boxing photos and pinned dollar bills, all of it candied by Christmas lights. To Sophie's credit, she liked it.

"Actually, I majored in marketing," Leonard explained, "at my dad's alma mater. It was the only way I could get away from Harvard. But I took all the TAPS courses I could. After college, I spent a few years in the corporate world. Hated it, of course. Then I saw that Central was holding auditions—"

"Central?"

"The Royal Central School of Speech and Drama in London. That year, their American auditions happened to be in Chicago. So I took one final flier on acting."

Given how eager she had seemed to have a drink, he was surprised she kept checking her phone, which she left out on the bar. Sometimes she would pick it up, thumb-tap with satanic speed, and send something off with a whiz before saying sorry reflexively, without contrition, all of which irritated him, especially since he didn't really want to be there, at least not with her. He tried to drink his beer quickly, but the faster he drank, the better he felt. It was Saturday night and the place was packed and they had to shout in each other's ear, shoulders pressed. This was the pleasure of a crowded bar, to be in your own little world in the midst of other people. Each time he leaned in, he felt her nearness, her presence, and he didn't really mind when she started brushing his knee. They ordered another round.

"Do you know who's in love with you?" he asked at one point, gleefully.

"Who?" she asked, wide-eyed.

"Ryan Gushiken!"

She punched him in the shoulder. "Shut *up!*"

A few beers in, *his* phone went off. A wonder he'd even felt it in all that clamor. His first thought was Emily—who else would be calling at that time of night?—and he felt a stab of guilt and elation, but the feeling was short-lived. A 617 number, only it wasn't his father. He was inclined to ignore it. Instead, he put a finger to his ear and answered. The man at the other end said he was Uncle Leung. Before Leonard realized who it was, the man said, "Leonard, it's your father."

———

The drive to Cambridge was bleary and dark, the highway a field of gauzy red stars. The roads unscrolled hypnotically, yellow dashes on one side, an endless white line on the other, and Leonard took them unconsciously, all the way to the Mass Pike without knowing how he'd gotten there, instinct at the wheel, his mind somewhere else.

As soon as he'd gotten off the phone, he'd walked out of the bar and called Emily. All these months of waffling and suddenly he was calling without a second thought. There was no answer, though—he imagined her rolling over in bed, shutting off her phone, and turning back to whoever—but he couldn't tell her like that, in a message, so he asked her to call him right away. By this point, Sophie had come outside, but he didn't want to tell her, either, not before he told Emily. "I'm sorry, I have to go to Cambridge" was all he said, and she nodded gingerly, catching on.

He had just seen his father earlier that week when he came to see *Lear*. His father had never had much to say about his shows—whether this was judgment, indifference, or ignorance, Leonard could never tell—but there his father was in the front row every year on opening night. After the show, he took his father drinking with the cast and crew and got him good and soused, which was fun, his father a merry drunk. In the morning, his father still got up early to do his stretches while Leonard tried to sleep it off. *"Wo zoule,"* his father said eventually. "Okay, see you, Dad," Leonard replied, an arm draped over his eyes. For a while, he felt his father standing there with his long face and long ears—Buddha ears, Leonard used to call them—and could see what his father must have seen, a man of nearly fifty splayed out on the couch, hungover, childless, ever floundering, and now on the cusp of divorce. He sensed that his father wanted to talk, but he staunchly refused to uncover his eyes. In time, the front door shut with a gentle click.

When Leonard had announced they were going to have a baby, his father had been surprisingly animated. They had been sitting on a bench on the grounds of his mother's nursing home, and his father had beamed, clapping his hands above his head.

"Here's the thing, though," Leonard said wretchedly. "Emily and I, we lost our insurance . . ."

He expected a lecture. Instead, his father tapped a fist to his chest, playfully, the way he used to when Leonard was a boy.

"Whatever you need."

———

Before he reached the Charles, he pulled off and got himself a room. What he'd needed, he realized, was some great expenditure—renting a car, leaving right away, plowing through the small hours—to make him feel less helpless, but now he wasn't ready to face whatever had to be faced. He hadn't brought anything with him, had gone straight from Jimmy's to the Enterprise down the street. So he brushed his teeth with his finger under sallow fluorescent light, in a motel bathroom lined with stained grout and poorly piped caulk. That's where he was, in a green-carpeted room darkened by blackout curtains, when Emily called in the morning.

"Sorry, I was asleep," she said.

When he broke the news, the line went still. "I'm coming right now."

He hadn't realized how much he needed to hear those words until she said them. When he hung up, he could hear his father chiding him for having to do what he hadn't been able to do himself: get her to come to him.

———

When he reached the house in West Cambridge, he sat for a while in the driveway. The house was a classic Cape, white with green shutters and two poky dormers, a garage appended to one side and a sunroom to the other. The sunroom was where his mother had liked to paint. For decades, it had been the tidiest of studios, her art paper stacked in folded sheets, like pastry dough, but in later years, after she had turned to abstraction, her mind going, her canvases had cluttered the room in long rows like sliced loaves of bread. Well before she died, he and his father had sorted through her things and gotten rid of most, but nothing about her dying had prepared him for this. Hers had been a slow leaching, a mercy in the end; his father's death was a blow.

At last he approached the house. When he opened the door, he caught a hint of something rank, above and beyond the taint of age. For the past ten years, his father had been retired. No more classes, no more meetings, no more research, just visits to the nursing home when his wife was still alive and regular appointments with friends. When he didn't show up for his weekly game of mahjong and wouldn't answer the phone, his friends came to check on him . . .

Leonard went through every room in the now-museum, opening windows. In the kitchen, where the faucet still had the same glass knobs he remembered from childhood, the *H* and the *C* in curlicue script, he shut off a slow drip. When he reached the master bedroom upstairs, its ceiling so pitched you had to duck to walk around the bed, he paused in the doorway. This was where his father was found, his shirt half-buttoned. What did he think about, getting ready for the day, and what did he think about, lying on the floor, his world upturned?

The room he came to last was his father's office on the ground floor, the room he hadn't been allowed to enter whenever his father was working, and the child in him still balked. The blinds were drawn, which made the room feel sheeted for winter. All of his father's shelves were devoted to books save for the one that housed every medal, plaque, and trophy that Leonard had collected as a child. On the wall behind his father's desk was a poster that read NEVER TRUST AN ATOM. THEY MAKE UP EVERYTHING. When Leonard was young, his father had taken him to see all kinds of spark chambers and particle accelerators, hoping to spark and accelerate something in his son, but nothing ever took. Instead, Leonard dreamed of completing that shelf with the golden statuette of a winged woman holding an atom above her head, or better yet, the one of a man holding a longsword atop a reel of film. But it never happened, and now it was too late.

———

Every hour or so, ellipses flashed on his phone like bulbs on a marquee, followed by a bloop and the name of a place: New Haven, Hartford, Worchester.

Around noon, as he sat on the front steps, a sporty red compact appeared at the end of the block. It couldn't have been going more than twenty, twenty-five miles an hour, but on that leafy street it appeared to be racing. With a bobble and a scrape, it turned into the driveway. In one motion, Emily shifted into park and opened the door and then she was running.

———

There weren't as many things to do as Leonard might have thought. He had spent the morning calling people, including Bex and Uncle Leung, who was coming over later, but it turned out his father had prearranged everything, for a lot of reasons, Leonard suspected. As a kindness, yes, but also because he knew his son wouldn't have the money, at least not enough to give him the kind of face he wanted.

So he and Emily sat in the sunroom, where time seemed elastic. He couldn't quite believe he had seen her last night, it seemed so long ago now. And he couldn't quite believe she was back—in his parents' house, no less. Then again, she'd been coming here for almost twenty years.

"Remember our first trip out east?" he asked.

"God, I was so nervous."

"Yeah, but my parents loved you. You were so . . . solicitous. And you knew to call them Mr. and Mrs. Xiao." After they were married, Emily had even called them "Mom" and "Dad," in Chinese fashion. "That kind of shit mattered."

She laughed, knees drawn to her chest.

"Did I ever tell you about Charlie Simpson?" he asked, alighting on a memory. "He was a friend of mine when I was a kid. Used to live over there," he said, pointing down the street. "His mother died when we were ten. Cancer, I think. Anyway, a few days later, he came over to play, but my mother sent him home. Said he couldn't come over for seven weeks."

Emily gave him a sad little frown.

"I know, right? Even then, I thought it was a lousy thing

to do. I mean, the poor kid had just lost his mother. But that kind of shit mattered, too."

"What did your dad say?"

"Nothing."

"How could he be so superstitious? He was a physicist."

"One of the mysteries of the universe. Me and Charlie were never straight after that."

He had to wonder if repeated experience like that hadn't made him quietly resolve *not* to be like his parents. Then again, maybe if he'd cared about those things, his luck would have been different.

———

In the afternoon, Uncle Leung and other friends of his parents came to the house to help make arrangements. The men were all of a piece with his father, college or army buddies whose families had also managed by some turn of fortune's wheel to cross the Taiwan Strait in the last days of the Chinese Civil War. Leonard had known these people all his life, had fallen asleep in their homes as a child to the sound of mahjong tiles clattering like rain. They were voluble, gracious, and warm to Emily, who had known them a long time herself, and he couldn't have been more relieved when they left.

Afterward, on the drive back from the rental agency where they dropped off her car, frugal as ever, Emily said, "I'm glad your dad had friends."

He knew what she meant. Still, a bitterness coursed through him. "Do you know who those people are? Those are the people who were always asking about me. Not because they cared. Because they wanted to brag. 'Our son just bought a house.' 'Our daughter just bought *us* a house.' Those are the people whose fucking feelings mattered to my parents."

Though he kept his eyes on the road, he felt hers thinning, and sensed her sensing a change, new yet darkly familiar.

At the end of the day, after they had eaten some of the food his parents' friends had brought over, he got out some pillows and bedding and made up the couch.

"Len," she said ruefully.

"What?" he asked, miffed. "Are you getting a room?"

"No, of course not. It's just—you didn't have to do that."

"It's no big deal," he said, still terse.

When he made for the couch, she said, "I'll sleep here."

"You can sleep up—"

"No, really."

She hurried under the blanket and pulled it up to her neck, with two hands, then searched him a little frantically. Was she worried he was going to try something? Force her to tell him the truth?

"Good night, Em."

He trudged upstairs to his old room and lay in the dark, aware of her presence, under the same roof for the first time in months, but it wasn't much of a balm. The house and its night sounds dredged up the past; the old tensions, the old quarrels—

You two just want an easy life!

Jesus Christ, Dad, you think our lives are easy?

After a while, footsteps creaked on the stairs and stopped outside his door. He could feel her on the other side, trying to catch the sound of his breathing. He thought about calling out but waited for her to call out first. Then, a barely perceptible shift of weight, the very beginning, it seemed, of a pivot, a turn, and he sat up and reached for the covers, ready to spring. But then, without a knock, the door opened, and she came to him. He didn't know why or what it meant, didn't know and didn't care. Pity, sorrow, guilt, reflex—any reason was good enough.

———

They woke up in a somber mood—today was the day. In the sunroom, they sat down to breakfast, fortifications. By the light of day, Leonard had to wonder if last night wasn't the same thing: the bookend on a life.

At one point, his phone whooshed. Bex with a sweet, thoughtful message and a picture of the final curtain call. Strange to think there had been a show last night, that it all went on without him. Then his phone rang.

"You got the callback!" Mackenzie screamed. "You nailed the demo! The CD *loved* you. Now she wants you to do it *exactly* the same for the director and the producers. No presh, but this could be big. For you *and* me."

Her voice was jarring. He didn't tell her where he was or what had happened, and he tried not to think about what he'd have to think about to do the scene *exactly*. But that old, implacable upswing—he couldn't help but feel it. Maybe his days of memorizing seven-hundred-plus lines were over, but he could still deliver a few at a time—

"Who was that?"

He played it up. This wasn't just another nibble, he tried to imply. This could finally be the big one. But her face curdled, and that long final day came back to him, and he knew their woes weren't over, that time had solved nothing.

He went inside to make himself another cup of coffee. Imagined his anger flowing into the Bialetti until it gurgled loudly on the stovetop. Then he went back out and took a thoughtless sip.

"Ow, fuck!"

"Goose," she said, smiling.

He tongued some loose skin on the inside of his lip. "It's not funny."

"Should have learned your lesson the first time."

"What are you talking about?"

"The first time you burned your mouth."

"When?"

"On your first cup!"

A frisson of alarm. "I did?"

She looked at him askance. "Don't be weird."

"I'm not."

She sat up. She'd been through it all before with his mother. Knew the signs.

"Len, what's going on?"

"I don't know."

"Have you seen a doctor?"

"I was waiting to get through the show."

"Have you been going up on your lines?"

He didn't answer. Leave it to her to notice.

She stood. "I'm calling right now."

———

All through the long day, first at the crematorium filled with standing wreaths draped in white naming banners, and then in the altar room at the only Chinese funeral parlor in Boston, where an urn with a locket-sized picture of his father sat on a table filled with food and joss paper, and then outside the funeral parlor, where the joss paper was burned in an iron stove, and finally at the cemetery, where his father was reunited with his mother—all through the day, Leonard kept thinking that he wasn't ready to go. Wasn't ready for it all to be over. At moments like this, when everything seemed so real, so manifestly *there*, it was hard to believe it would ever have to end. That the world, the whole show, would go on without him.

His parents' plot lay in the shadow of a burning sugar maple, the grounds so lovely that people cycled and picnicked there, just because. After a groundskeeper had removed the granite slab atop the urn vault, Leonard placed his father's urn next to his mother's. Once the slab was returned, Emily put a hand on his shoulder and said, "Take your time," and he found himself alone before a new headstone, engraved with words he couldn't read. Most of the day, he wouldn't have known exactly what to do if not for his parents' friends, but he knew what to do now. When his mother was laid to rest, he had kowtowed three times, so he got down on his knees and touched his head to the ground. Prostrate, as he'd never been in life.

I'm sorry, I tried. I really did.

He sat up a little too quickly and gave himself a head rush. Hadn't eaten in a while, he realized.

He lowered his head again, his throat stinging. Wished they had had that talk.

I don't know what to do.

He sat up again, slowly this time. Saw his father, clear as day, clapping his hands above his head. Then Leonard touched his head to the ground for the third and final time, and kept it down, in a cool tangle of grass, eyes burning.

Jesus Christ, Dad.

———

That night, they lay in bed, in the unconsoling dark, sapped but also wired, minds still revolving. Now that one hard thing was over, Leonard tried to turn to the next.

"I own this house," he said. He waited for her to take exception—"*We* own this house"—but she didn't.

"Are you going to live here?"

He imagined living in the house as it was. Then he imagined taking it down to the studs. Both seemed unthinkable.

"I spent my whole life trying to get away. Not sure I can come back."

"What are you going to do, then?"

"If I rent it out, I could get a better place in the city—"

She tensed.

"—or maybe I should sell and buy somewhere else."

"Where?"

"I don't know."

Each of them tried to picture where that place might be. Or maybe that wasn't it. Maybe she was thinking about something—or someone—else.

"Just tell me, do you love him?"

She didn't turn or flinch, just stared at the space above her, eyelids flapping languidly, like slow-beating wings. The fact that she wouldn't answer was all the answer he needed.

———

Years ago, as pale wintry light shone on the painted tarmac of what were normally basketball courts, Leonard and Emily had wandered the tented tables of GreenFlea Market, which sat in the shadow of low-rise apartments on the Upper West Side, their fire escapes zigging and zagging.

Emily was pregnant and starting to show, but you couldn't tell in her puffy jacket.

Normally, flea markets put him in happy scavenger mode, especially when he was with Emily, who had that eye, but that day he felt a little depressed, thinking of their baby in a secondhand crib, a secondhand carrier, riding the faded tail of other people's cometing hopes. But then, in the midst of his gloom, he came across a little painting, maybe a foot square. A rainbow of elephants in profile, joined in a circle, nose to tail. The elephants lay on a white background, and the whole thing sat in a gilded frame.

"What do you think of this?" he asked, holding up the painting.

Her eyelids went sleepy with happiness. "It's perfect."

———

They drove back to the city the next day. Harvard was planning a memorial service at the Faculty Club, but that wouldn't be for a while yet. Despite a low ceiling of cloud, Leonard stayed hidden behind his sunglasses. When they reached the city, Emily directed him to a brownstone he'd never seen in Park Slope.

During the drive, Leonard kept rehearsing the things he wanted to say, things he'd started to hatch in the small hours of night, Emily sleeping beside him, but it wasn't until they hit I-95 in Connecticut that he finally said, "I called my agent this morning. I'm not going in for the callback. I told her my father died, so she wouldn't be mad. Or *as* mad." He saw his old self slipping away on a fast-moving ice floe. "All these years, I've been carrying this weight, this burden, you know? It didn't make my parents happy, it didn't make you happy, and I'm not even sure it made *me* happy. But now I realize I don't have to carry it. I can just set it down, and the world will go on. So that's what I'm going to do. I did my best. Did some decent work. I can live with that. I've got nothing left to prove—and no one left to prove it to." Which wasn't true. He had always wanted to prove it to *her*. "Okay, so I didn't get everything I wanted. But it's not too late for other things. I'm sorry I couldn't go back to my dad after we lost the baby. I'm sorry we didn't try every last thing. But now we can. Forty-two isn't too late. We can sell the house and spend every last dollar if we have to. Even in the worst-case scenario, I'll still have a few good years. That baby will know me, and I swear I'll know that baby." This part he believed, truly. "Maybe we'll even have time for more than one. Or better yet, maybe we'll have twins—or triplets. That's how these things go, right? When it rains, it pours. We still have time. To make things right."

Leonard had kept his eyes on the road, but now he braved a look. Emily was dabbing her face with the heels of her hands—and not for the first time, he didn't know why.

———

He dropped off his rental car in Times Square, then took the N train to Chinatown. From the station, he walked to Elizabeth Street and sat down in a greasy spoon, the kind with disposable white tablecloths, thin and slick as garbage bags. This might have been the place that he and Emily had gone to on their very first night in the city, but honestly, he couldn't remember.

He ordered in English, pointing at the menu. A bowl of congee with pork and century egg—classic breakfast fare, comfort food. When he took his first unthinking bite, he got a swift and powerful waft of childhood. Something to do with the egg, maybe, brown with black yolk and smelling of sulfur. Suddenly he was a boy again, being called down to dinner in Cambridge. Maybe his favorite time of day, when he got to see what his parents had made. His job was to scoop rice from a green Tatung rice cooker, whose metal lid rattled as steam escaped and whose lever popped up when the rice was done. He hadn't thought of these things in years, but it all came back to him now.

After his mother moved into the nursing home, he and Emily had gone to help his father sort through her things. When Leonard said, "These are cool. I'll take these," holding up a couple of his mother's "Kandinskys," his father had whipped around, eyes raw, and asked, "Why don't you like her *good* paintings?" meaning, *Why can't you be more Chinese?* At the time, the accusation had chafed, but now he saw that his father was right. All his life, he'd been acting. All his life, he'd been forgetting.

——

Two days after getting back to the city, Leonard stood in the kitchen, pushing a knife through the plasticky skin of an avocado and running it around the pit before prying the halves apart. With a gentle squeeze, he urged the pit from the half it was stuck to, then pried it out with a spoon, leaving a perfectly unmarred impression in the perfectly ripened flesh. After ladling the flesh with long, deep scoops, he turtled the halves on the cutting board and sliced with buttery ease. What a pleasure, being alive. Having a mind. Since coming back from Cambridge, he'd felt more sanguine. All those little blips during the show, were they really anything new? You couldn't be an actor without forgetting your lines. Likely he always had, only time had sanded the edges. And that moment with the coffee. Well, he'd been grieving—was still grieving— and grief did strange and terrible things. If someone had asked, he would have said he would live another forty-eight years.

As he dumped cubes of avocado into a bowl, his phone whooshed.

U were right. Ryan G ♥ me!!!

He burst out laughing. Hands dirty, he pinky typed:

Told you.

She replied:

Will spill when I see u.

Yesterday, Sophie had messaged to say that she'd found an apartment. She was going to chase the dream right here in the mecca, and he'd felt such pity and envy. To be young again. To have it all before you. In the past twenty years, the industry had started to change for actors like them. Slowly, to be sure, but not imperceptibly. She had a chance, and he quietly wished her lucky passage.

Where's your place?

he'd asked.

Wash Heights ☺

He'd sent back the astonished emoji.

Let's have dinner, Len. We're neighbors!!!

He had spent the morning on his hands and knees, deep cleaning the apartment. It was an annual rite, getting things back in order after the chaos of the run. In the afternoon, he went shopping for dinner. He was trying a new dish, tostones with shrimp-and-avocado salad. He went all the way to Little Senegal for plantains and all the way to Dorian's for shrimp. It was fun to go to extravagant lengths, just to say he had. Fun to be dating again.

He tossed the avocado with the shrimp, along with tomato, red onion, cilantro, jalapeño, and lime juice, and put it all in the fridge to chill. Just as he stuck the tip of his knife into a green plantain, he heard someone at the door. He'd left the door unlocked. It was coy of her to knock.

He opened the door and there she was.

"Hi, Em."

———

A few days later, they sat in the waiting room of his GP on West 147th Street. This was the first appointment Emily had been able to get for him. The first thing his doctor was going to want, Leonard knew, was an MRI. Only if it came back clean would she send him to see a neurologist. It would be a while yet before anyone knew anything for certain.

"Look who's splitting up," Emily said, holding out a dated copy of a tabloid magazine.

A chanteuse who'd gone on to voice a Disney movie and an alt country singer they both happened to like. "That's too bad," he said.

"Fame," she replied, shaking her head.

In the past week, they'd had dinner twice. The first time, she came to his place. The second time, they went to Ponty Bistro in Harlem, where Emily had a Niçoise salad, sitting against a big tufted backrest. Both times, she had spent the night. She hadn't said anything yet about who-ever he had seen her with and didn't seem curious to know how he knew. He hoped they would soon be sitting in other waiting rooms, for the reasons he'd proposed, but she hadn't said anything about that, either. But he didn't care. She was making time.

Eventually a door to the waiting room opened and a heavyset nurse appeared.

"Leonard Xiao?" she asked, casting her glance about.

He rose and started toward her and was almost at the door when he realized he was alone. He swung around, panicked. Was she not coming in?

When Emily saw his addled look, she smiled.

"Don't worry," she said. "I'll be right here."

No, no, no, no. Come, let's away to prison.
We two alone will sing like birds i' th' cage.
When thou dost ask me blessing, I'll kneel down
And ask of thee forgiveness; so we'll live,
And pray, and sing, and tell old tales, and laugh
At gilded butterflies, and hear poor rogues
Talk of court news, and we'll talk with them too—
Who loses and who wins, who's in, who's out,
And take upon 's the mystery of things
As if we were God's spies

                           let's   to prison.
We two alone will sing   i' th' cage.
When   dost ask   blessing, I'll
        ask   forgiveness;   we'll live,
                and sing   old tales, and laugh
At gilded butterflies, and   poor rogues
                           and we'll talk with them too—
        loses and   wins,
                      the mystery of things
                      spies

We two

rogues

Acknowledgments

MY GRATITUDE TO MY AGENT, JACKIE KAISER OF WESTWOOD Creative Artists, and everyone at HarperVia, especially Tara Parsons, Judith Curr, John McGhee, and Stephen Brayda. To Andrea Wan for the beautiful cover art. Gratitude to the whole team at House of Anansi Press in Canada, especially Sarah MacLachlan, Janie Yoon, Maria Golikova, Sonya Lalli, Alysia Shewchuk, and Gil Adamson. Many thanks to Ithaca College and the David T. K. Wong Creative Writing Fellowship at the University of East Anglia. Thanks to the judges of the 2014 Commonwealth Short Story Prize and the 2017 Writers' Trust McClelland & Stewart Journey Prize, as well as the literary journals and anthologies that published my stories and the editors who made them better: Kevin Chong, Pamela Mulloy, Ellah Wakatama Allfrey,

John Barton, Anita Chong, and Jasmine Sealy. Of the many sources consulted in the writing of these stories, I would particularly like to acknowledge *Saltwater City: An Illustrated History of the Chinese in Vancouver* by Paul Yee, *Women on Ice: The Early Years of Women's Hockey in Western Canada* by Wayne Norton, *My Forty Years as a Diplomat* by Feng-shan Ho, *Several Worlds: Reminiscences and Reflections of a Chinese-American Physician* by Monto Ho, and *Colour, Confusion and Concessions: The History of the Chinese in South Africa* by Melanie Yap and Dianne Leong Man. Thanks to those who read my work-in-progress, especially Eleanor Henderson, Jacob White, Raul Palma, Gabriel Urza, Yewande Omotoso, Mahreen Sohail, Henrietta Rose-Innes, and Tracey Iceton—and thanks to Courtney Young for sharing her experiences as an actor in New York City. Thanks as well to my parents; my brother, Holman; my daughters, Zadie and Zoe; and Po, my late maternal grandmother, to whom "The Nature of Things" is dedicated. Thanks above all to my wife, Angelina, for love, time, and patience.

Here ends Jack Wang's
We Two Alone.

The first edition of this book was printed and
bound at LSC Communications in
Harrisonburg, Virginia, May 2021.

A NOTE ON THE TYPE

The text of this book was set in Dante, a typeface
designed by Giovanni Mardersteig after the end of
World War II, when his private press Officina Bodoni
resumed operations. Influenced by the Monotype
Bembo and Centaur typefaces, Mardersteig wanted
to design a font that balanced italic and roman harmo-
niously. Originally hand-cut by Charles Malin, it was
adapted for mechanical composition by Monotype
in 1957. Dante remains a popular typeface today, and
it appears especially elegant on the printed page.

HARPERVIA

An imprint dedicated to publishing international voices,
offering readers a chance to encounter other lives and other
points of view via the language of the imagination.